With the heat of the sun warm on her cheeks, Cindy sadly gazed out over the valley below. If only she had someone to share the moment, her life would be complete. But here, in quiet solitude, she finally admitted to herself how much the last few weeks had hurt. The shock of Brent's unfaithfulness had wrenched her from a storybook world and left her filled with pain and bitter disillusionment.

Brent of the laughing eyes and wicked smile, whose face appeared in her mind and sent hurt surging through her heart. Cindy had always known that he was attractive to other women; but she had always been proud in the knowledge her handsome fiance was true.

She remembered the scene clearly, bitterly. She had come home with the groceries to find Brent and a scantily clad girl, his arms around her. And then the confrontation . . . .

No, Cindy told herself now, she must forget it—she must forget Brent. But she knew it would not be easy.

A Tiara Romance

SPITFIRE

Barbara Phillips

Ace/Stoneshire Books London

Dedicated to Linda DuBreuil, and to Dave and the kids

First Published in the U.S.A. by
Nordon Publications Inc.

© 1981 by Barbara Phillips

First Ace/Stoneshire Paperback 1983

Printed in the U.K.

ONE

The incline had been long and gradual, and although Cindy had kept a steady pressure of her foot against the accelerator, she'd almost forgotten that she'd been steadily climbing for several minutes, so the sudden descent caught her unawares. No highway sign had been erected to warn her to decrease her speed, but she'd already noticed the lack of such signs along the Kentucky road so she couldn't really excuse herself for not being prepared, she thought grimly as she sped downward. Her slender foot braked intermittently as she concentrated on keeping her small white sports car on the road.

The hill was abrupt and full of dangerous curves, but her mind was quick as she remembered not to ride the brakes or use too much force. To do so could have sent her spinning crazily off the road and down several hundred feet. She'd started out with the top down, and her long auburn hair blew straight behind her from beneath the brim of her large hat. The rush of wind was a roar in her ears as she rounded a final curve and felt her heart in her mouth.

Only by the grace of God had she avoided hitting someone. He was there in front of her car, a short, slightly bowlegged figure that moved quickly to the side of the road to avoid getting killed, she realized as she sped on by. Out of the corner of her eye she saw vague outlines of other men too, wondered what they'd been doing there on an isolated strip of country road, then realized that at least one of them had yelled at her. Something about keeping her kiddy car off the road before she killed someone.

She looked into the rear-view mirror as she passed a clump of trees, and saw several bright, red-jacketed figures. Her cheeks grew almost as red as the jackets when she realized she'd come close to killing a group of men who were surveying the road. "Lord!" The exclamation came out in a half sob as the trees hid the road crew from her sight. "Lord!" She said it again as she crawled along at ten miles an hour, thankful that she'd made it down the hill without killing someone—or herself.

A wishing well, constructed of rock and with a dilapidated wooden covering, was on the right-hand side of the road, and Cindy Kelly remember-ed the map the real estate people had given her, along with notations of landmarks. She didn't have to look at the map to remember the wishing well, which would be followed by an old covered bridge. And the bridge was straight ahead. Still maintaining her speed of ten miles an hour, she held her breath while she drove over the creaking, groaning planks, and heaved a sigh of relief once she was safely across. Less than thirty feet away was the narrow lane she'd been instructed to look for. After she turned into the lane and brought her car to a halt in a clearing, she sat and stared with wide eyes at the sight before her.

"Oh, no," she moaned, "I've really done it now!"

Cindy was twenty-three, and all of those years had been spent living in the city. But even from her earliest memories her most passionate dream was to live in the country, to have animals, and to grow things in rich black earth. She had never liked the city—the tall buildings, the concrete sidewalks and the noisy traffic. Her father used to tell her she had inherited her dreams from her grandmother, who came to the city as a bride and never stopped yearning for the peace and quiet of the country. Maybe so; she remembered all the wonderful stories of country living her grandmother had told her long ago. And she, a dreamy, enchanted child, would say, "When I grow up, Grandma, I'm going to get married and live in the country!" And her round child's eyes would glow.

Now, years later, Grandma was gone but the dream was still there, although after her engagement she had allowed it to be pushed into a distant future. Brent, her fiance, had never understood the longing she had had for the simple life, but he had allowed her to believe that some day they would live away from the city. Of course he had told her it would be awhile before they could afford a place like that, and in the meanwhile they would live in an apartment and work in the teeming town.

Cindy had pushed the idea of gardens and farm animals to the back of her mind and replaced it with windowboxes of flowers and Tabby, her cat. And somehow she succeeded in stifling her dreams more and more. It really didn't matter where you lived, she'd told herself, as long as you're with the one you love.

But that love had been shaken to its very foundations when she'd been faced with Brent's unfaithfulness. Seeking relief from the shattering blow, her mind had turned to her dream more and more. Slowly it became an obsession.

Then a listing had come into the real estate agency where she worked. It told in grand and flowery detail of a small cabin located about fifty miles south of Lexington—an ideal place for someone seeking solitude, and a handyman's paradise, it had gone on to say.

Cindy had worked at the agency long enough to recognize the phrase "handyman's paradise." Extensive repairs would be required. But still the idea of that cabin haunted her and her mind churned with an impulsive idea. If she didn't do it now, she never would, she told herself. Quickly she ran to the bank, withdrew her savings and plunked them down on the little farm. The papers were signed, the place was hers. There wasn't any way she could talk herself out of it then!

The following day Cindy informed her employer of her purchase and requested an early vacation. She'd assured him she would keep her job. The farm was not very far away; she would commute. She had been surprised at his relief; she'd never realized how much he depended on her. She'd known her work was satisfactory, but she was surprised to hear him speak of her competence in glowing terms.

Remembering the mess the last girl had left, and the thought of trying to find someone new to fill Cindy's shoes, had left small, portly Mr. Ames in a panic. Hovering over her, he'd patted her shoulder compassionately as he stated, "We've all noticed how unhappy you've been lately. And although we don't know what your problems are, we wish the best for you. Enjoy your vacation by all means, and come back to us the happy, cheerful person you were before. Okay?"

Touched, she had accepted the three weeks' leave and the good wishes of her coworkers. She promised invitations to them all as soon as she had the cabin fit for company.

A day later she'd loaded her car with her most necessary items, and as an added thought had tied a box of her red geraniums among the provisions. Flowers from her old home to her new, she'd told herself whimsically. Laughing at herself, Cindy had settled Tabby, the calico cat, on the seat beside her.

Then came the saddest part of all—leaving her parents and the home which had been hers for twenty-three years, and starting out on her own. They had all managed to keep stiff upper lips, but parting was hard. After many promises of letters, and a visit in three weeks, Cindy kissed her parents goodby. And with great expectations she'd headed south.

Now here she was, staring in silence at the rustic hideaway for which she had spent her savings. Misgivings whirling in her head, she slowly opened the door of the car and with wide incredulous eyes stared at the forlorn little cabin. *This was the scenic mountain farm she'd bought?* The roof of the porch sagged alarmingly, the post leaning so far over that a strong gust of wind would surely make the whole thing a shambles. With dismay she saw that the windows contained nothing but shattered panes of glass. Wild grass covered the sloping yard, weeds and wild flowers grew in profusion.

Beside her, Tabby slowly arose and stretched

with dignity, then strutted from the car and disappeared into the thick grass. She was going to investigate. Biting her full upper lip, Cindy flipped the large hat from her head and onto the seat of the car. She might as well look around, too, she decided.

Cautiously she picked her way past the dangerously sagging old fence that surrounded the cabin. With care she gingerly stepped through the high grass and up to the porch, still keeping a watchful eye. There was always a danger from poisonous snakes in this neck of the woods, she warned herself.

Mutely she inspected the sagging porch and decided she'd be much safer to use the back door. "Thank heavens I'm not fainthearted," she muttered aloud. "Otherwise I'd drive back to the city without a look!"

As she rounded the corner, Cindy halted in midstride, slowly removed her sunglasses, and, with a sigh, gazed at the breathtaking view to her right. The cabin was situated on a high hill that looked out over the valley. The trees were a kaleidoscope of fall colors. Down at the end of the valley, in the far distance, a small white church with a tall steeple gleamed in the September sun, so distant it looked like a child's toy. In that moment she fell in love with the little mountain farm. As she breathed in the clear fresh air she was aware of birds singing and the rustle of trees in the gentle wind.

With the heat of the sun warm on her cheeks, Cindy sadly gazed out over the valley below. If she had someone to share the enjoyment of the moment, her life would be complete. Only here, in quiet solitude, would she admit how much the last few weeks had hurt. The shock of Brent's unfaithfulness had wrenched her from a storybook world and left her filled with pain and bitter disillusionment. This place, she felt, would be a balm to her shattered pride and help her come to some decision about Brent.

Brent of the laughing eyes and wicked smile, whose face appeared in her mind and sent hurt surging through her heart. Cindy had always known of the attention Brent drew from other women and she had laughed when he flirted outrageously. But she was sure he'd always be true and it had been a source of pride to her that her fiance was so handsome and desirable.

Then came the day she'd left work early to surprise Brent with a romantic dinner at the apartment they'd rented together, the place where they planned to be so happy. But the surprise had been on her, she remembered bitterly. She'd clutched the bag of groceries under one arm as she put the key in the lock, and smiled in anticipation of the night that lay ahead.

The door swung open and she stepped into the room. Then her smile faltered and slowly faded and her eyes filled with pain at the scene before her. It was as though it were a frame in a movie and the film had broken, the characters frozen into position. *She*, standing in the open door, the bag of groceries in her arms. And *Brent*, staring into her shocked eyes over the shoulder of the scantily clad young woman he held in his arms.

"Cindy . . . ." His tone was chagrined, and he'd hastily pulled the girl's clinging arms from his neck and started toward her, his hands raised in supplication. "This isn't what it appears to be. I . . . I . . . uh . . . she's our neighbor . . . from down

11

the hall. She just came to show me where the fuse box is."

"Don't, Brent, don't," she said numbly, as she stared down at the bag in her arms. Oddly, she found herself wondering if the frozen vegetables were beginning to thaw. It was as though the groceries were her only realities in the nightmare situation; her mind refused to cope with anything more.

"Don't lie to her, Brent," the lithe brunette advised with calm detachment as she slipped into her clothes. "I'm glad she knows."

"Get out of here," Brent blazed, furious at her words.

"I'm going, darling." She smiled boldly, "But if things don't work out, you know where to find me." Then, with an air of assurance, she picked up her purse, hooked it over her shoulder and walked to the door. Briefly she hesitated, and Cindy could see a touch of pity in her dark eyes. "A word of advice, my dear," she said. "Never trust his kind. They always let you down." Then the door opened and she was gone, the click of her heels echoing in the hall.

Silently Cindy carried the bag into the small kitchen and mechanically set about putting the food away. The vegetables had started to melt and it seemed to be of the utmost importance that she get them into the freezer.

Brent's eyes were anxious as he took the dripping packages from her hands and laid them aside. "Cindy, for God's sake," he beseeched, "say something. Don't leave me dangling."

It exploded inside her. The sheer physical force of her pain drove the breath from her lungs and she was surprised to find that she was laughing uncontrollably. "Leave . . . you . . . dangling . . . ." she gasped, between peals of bitter mirth. "I would say I'm the one dangling. And the sad part is, I never suspected."

"Cindy, don't look at me like this," he begged. "I didn't think you'd ever find out. It was only a fling before we were married. I don't want her. She means nothing to me."

The laughter had trailed away and her emotions had frozen into an icy calm. "Does anything have meaning for you, Brent?" she asked as she turned away.

"Of course it does," he said passionately. "I want us to be together. That means more to me than you'll ever know."

A cold rage had enveloped her and she wanted to hit him, hurt him as he had hurt her. "You have a funny way of showing how much you care," she said bitterly.

The look Brent turned upon her was amazing. It held a slight tinge of shame, but most of all it held confidence. He was sure she'd forgive him; she could see it in his eyes.

"You're upset and you're making more out of this than you should," he said. "Every man alive has stepped out of line at one time or another."

"You're wrong, Brent." Cindy's voice trembled. "Some men are faithful. Some men wouldn't stoop to this kind of deceit."

"Aw, now, Cindy. I know it looks bad," he wheedled with boyish charm. "But after you've calmed down a bit you'll see that our relationship is as strong as ever."

The audacity of his remark, and his presumption that all would be forgiven, overwhelmed her and she shook her head. "Our relationship is finished, Brent. I could never marry a man I didn't trust."

"You don't mean this." He was unbelieving as he stared at her. "You can't decide to throw everything away in just these few moments. What of all our plans? You can't do this!"

"You should have thought of that before," she said, as her throat tightened painfully. She fumbled with the engagement ring she wore on her finger. "Take back your ring; I don't want it any more."

"No, I won't accept it! You're making a decision that our lives depend on," he said, turning to the window. "At least think about it. This was my first mistake and it will never happen again, I swear."

"I believe you mean it now, but what happens the next time you're tempted?" Her voice was ragged and shaking. "It was bad enough that you were having an affair, but you brought her here. *Here* to our apartment, Brent!"

"Cindy, she lives next door. She was helping me with the fuse. I didn't bring her over here for that."

The rage had settled and now there was a danger that she might cry. The apartment was closing in on her and she wanted to get away before she broke down completely. Until this moment she'd held on, strengthened by the force of her anger. But now that it was gone, she was afraid her pride would be next.

"I must go." She fought back scalding tears. "I need time to think." Blindly she turned toward the door, and then she stopped. "Maybe you're right. Maybe I shouldn't decide now."

She refused to allow her tears to escape. That would be a sure sign of weakness, she told herself.

Brent wasn't worth it. The wound was fresh in her mind and at this moment she didn't believe it would ever heal.

She had left the building without looking back. The hurt and pain had blinded her to her surroundings and she walked down the street in a daze. She'd never been sure how she managed to get home, but she had.

She moved like an automaton through the days that followed, and the nights were spent in despair. Visions of Brent and the girl haunted her every waking moment and still she denied herself the relief that tears might bring. Gradually she had become a pale ghost of herself, never smiling and never forgetting.

Although her parents exchanged worried glances, they'd wisely kept quiet, hoping she'd confide in them when she was ready. But matters were brought into the open the night her mother rapped softly at her bedroom door. "Cindy, there's a phone call for you. It's Brent."

"Tell him I'm not here," Cindy replied wildly. "Tell him I don't want to speak to him, and tell him not to call any more."

"Cindy," her mother said firmly, "get hold of yourself. I'll take care of Brent, and then you and I are going to talk."

A few minutes later her mother was seated on her bed. "Now what's happened between you two?"

"Not much." Cindy laughed bitterly. "I surprised Brent last week by arriving at the apartment unannounced. He wasn't alone."

She saw her mother wasn't surprised. "So now you've decided to stop living? I thought you were stronger than that. Are you going to spend the rest of your days mired in self-pity because Brent was unfaithful? A lot of women have faced that problem. Some have walked away, and some forgive and forget. You must realize that the two go together. If you decide to continue the relationship the past must be buried. It would never work otherwise."

"Do you think I should forgive him?" Cindy's uncertainty revealed her inner turmoil.

"I can't advise you, Cindy," her mother replied gently. "You're the only one who knows."

"As usual you're right, Mom." Cindy smiled wanly. "I'm going to think about it awhile. I want to be sure, but I'm not going to sit around feeling sorry for myself any more. The next time Brent calls I'll talk to him."

A few days later Brent called again, and at the sound of his voice she realized she still carried deep feelings for him in her heart. His pleas awakened a response and she wondered if her love was strong enough to heal the hurt. She wasn't sure. But she did find herself promising to think about forgiving him, and she agreed to keep his ring until she made her decision. She'd keep the ring, she told him, but she wouldn't wear it until she was sure she could put it on without qualms. She had lost all trust in him and, unless she could regain it, there would be nothing for them. Brent had argued and pleaded, but to no avail; Cindy was adamant, and he'd reluctantly agreed. She was confused and angry. She needed time to sort out her thoughts. How could she ever trust any man again?

Sighing, Cindy pushed the aching thoughts from her. She was determined not to dwell on unpleasant memories, and this ramshackle little place would provide enough work to keep her occupied for some time to come. At least it was one bright spot in her badly tarnished world.

After walking through the small three-room cabin and making a list of all the things she'd need, Cindy returned to town, which she'd driven through on her way to her place. There she found a motel on the outskirts.

"Yes," the talkative old man at the desk assured her, "we have vacancies. Of course you're lucky. The men from the survey company had all the rooms, but they left for Lexington just a little while ago and won't be back until next week."

Cindy had a questioning look on her face as she started to ask about the survey crew. But just as she began, he spoke up. "New highway comin' in. Bring in the tourists, yes, sir! Might even put this little ole town on the map!"

Cindy had different ideas on the subject, and she opened her mouth to tell him how she felt, how all the rustic qualities of the town might be lost because of commercialism and tourists. She wanted to tell him how much she liked the quiet, restful atmosphere. But again he stopped her before she could utter a word.

"Bought the old Jenkins place, eh?"

At her nod, he rambled on about her neighbors and the farms near her place, until her brain was whirling. She picked up her key and edged backward. It seemed as though she had gotten him started and he would never stop. Finally she made it through the door and, smiling ruefully, she hurried to her room.

Settling into bed that night, she knew she would never fall asleep. So she was surprised to awake early the next morning and know she had drifted off as soon as her head touched the pillow. It must be the fresh country air, she decided as she ran her fingers through her red-gold curls, yawning. Jumping from the bed, she stretched her slim supple body.

Quiet happiness washed over her as she anticipated her cabin in the pines. And she was surprised to realize she had passed the night without one disquieting thought of Brent. Quickly she resisted ideas of him, shoving him into the back of her mind. She would think about him later, after the hurt had faded a little and she could see with a clear mind. Until then, she would concentrate on fixing up her farm. And she'd be damned if she let thoughts of Brent spoil it for her!

As she showered, Cindy hummed softly. Later, planning for the work ahead, she dug through her suitcase and, with a triumphant cry pulled out a pair of faded jeans and a green-and-white checked shirt. Carelessly she pulled the copper-colored curls into a ponytail and grinned at her reflection in the mirror; she was beginning to look like a farm girl already!

Leaving the motel, Cindy moved hurriedly to her car, knowing that if the talkative little owner saw her she would never be able to break away. Luckily there was no sign of him and she made it out of the parking space and headed to town.

At the main street Cindy saw a sign: "Pine Valley. Population 389." It was now 390, she thought with satisfaction. And she was going to love living here. On her right was a hardware store. With her list in her hand, she entered.

"Yes, may I help you?" a friendly voice inquired. Turning around, Cindy saw a short, plump, smiling girl. Whom she instinctively liked.

"Hi, I'm Cindy Kelly," she said. "I've bought the old Jenkins place outside of town, and I sure could use some help. I need someone who does repairs and odd jobs. Do you know anyone who hires out for this kind of work?"

"Boy, are you wound up," the girl said. "I'm Jan Jenkins and that was my uncle's place you bought. And do you have a mess to clean up!"

"I know, but I love it there."

"Are you going to live up there *alone*?" Jan asked incredulously. "That's ten miles from town! No one even lives close to you."

"I know," Cindy replied calmly, "but that's one of the reasons I want it. I've always lived in apartments, with people all around. Now I want to enjoy spreading out. My grandmother came from a small town like this and she loved it. She always told me people were friendlier away from the city, and now I believe it." She smiled happily.

"After living in the city, the life here is pretty dull," Jan told her with a doubtful look.

"Oh, no!" Cindy assured her. "I find this very exciting."

"Exciting?" Jan looked doubtful. "I'll never understand city people."

"Don't call me city people," Cindy said with a little laugh. "I'm all country girl at heart."

Jan gave her an understanding smile. "You've already made quite an impression on several of the townsfolk."

"But I just arrived! I don't see how I could have made an impression on any—"

The other girl's pleasant laughter interrupted her. "You have a lot to learn about small towns, Cindy. Even though nobody knew your name until about five minutes after you registered at the motel, everyone in town, or at least most of us, knew you'd arrived. The men who were working on the road wasted no time about getting into town to describe the way you went down the hill like a bat out of hell and came close to taking several of them with you."

"Oh, dear."

"Well, they're men," Jan said with a humorous twist of her lips. "So they love it when they can put down a woman driver." Her friendly eyes sparkled. "But even though they made no bones about the way you were speeding down the hill, you made quite an impression on at least one of them." Her voice dropped. "He's Jed McCord and the women around town aren't doing a thing to put a dent in his king-sized ego, if you know what I mean. Lord, they flock after him in droves! Not that he's not rich, handsome, intelligent and—well, he's got everything in the world going for him, and to top it off, he's single! There aren't many eligible men around town, and Jed McCord is more eligible than most. Only thing is, he knows it. So everyone is biding his time, waiting for the two of you to get together."

"I hope no one holds his breath," Cindy said acidly. "Anyway, if he's all that great, why aren't you among the flocking females?"

Jan laughed. "Oh, I'm already spoken for." She held up her hand and Cindy admired a lovely diamond.

"It's beautiful," Cindy said. "I hope you'll be very happy."

The other girl's eyes lingered on the fourth finger of Cindy's left hand. "You've got a nice tan. Looks as if you've recently removed a ring from

20

your own finger."

Without thinking, Cindy glanced at her ring finger and the telltale band of white skin where her engagement ring had protected it from the sun. "I think maybe we'd best get back to my problems with the house," she said a trifle breathlessly. It just wasn't the time to talk about the diamond that rested inside the velvet box.

"Okay," answered Jan Jenkins. "Charlie over there—" she pointed—"does the kind of work you want done, and I'm sure he will help you out. Now give me your list. Glass for the windows, nails, paint, broom, mop, et cetera." She read aloud. "Come along. We have all this, even the et cetera."

After loading down the small car and making arrangements for Charlie to follow her to the cabin, Cindy squeezed herself into the jampacked seat, waved goodby to Jan Jenkins and headed down the road to her new home.

Cindy soon discovered that Charlie was a taciturn man. Although he was extremely capable, he wasted no time on small talk, but gathered up his tools and headed straight to the sagging porch. In no time at all the crooked post was braced and the little cabin seemed to straighten up at once.

Seeing that Charlie needed no help, Cindy squared her shoulders, tied the tails of her green-and-white shirt at her midriff, grabbed her mop and broom and, with a determined look in her eye, headed for the cabin. "Okay, Charlie," she called over her shoulder, "you take care of the outside and I'll take care of the inside."

"Yep," Charlie replied with a nod.

Cindy pushed the front door wide and ran full face into a huge spiderweb. Stifling a scream, she grabbed wildly at her hair. The idea of a spider crawling around on her almost threw her into a panic, no matter how many times she told herself to calm down. No little old spider was going to scare her away from the tasks at hand! She attacked all the cobwebs with the business end of the broom, before she felt safe enough to clean. After that, she worked diligently, taking great satisfaction in the changes made by soap, water and hard work.

Finding the rain barrel was a shock to her system. She hadn't realized that the only water supply on her little place was a tiny spring and the creek which flowed past her barn and down into the valley. But when she mentioned to Charlie the lack of modern plumbing, he merely shrugged. The sun would soon be setting and she was dogtired. Her voice was weak when she made arrangements with the handyman for what time to start work the following morning. But, worn out as she was, she retained a sense of deep satisfaction as she headed back toward town.

When morning came Cindy was already at the cabin before Charlie arrived. Her hair was tied back in a bandanna, her green eyes were sparkling as she painted the bedroom walls. "Hi," she said to Charlie when he entered and surveyed her work in his usual noncommittal way. "You know, I believe I'll be able to move in tomorrow."

"Ummm." Charlie turned away, and she wondered whether the "Ummm" meant that it was all right with him if she wanted to move in tomorrow or if it meant that he didn't much care for her choice of color. Within minutes his hammer sounded as he made further repairs, and it wasn't until she asked him if he'd like to share the lunch she'd brought from the motel that they exchanged another word.

He said, "Don't care much for boughten food, thanky kindly." Then he went off to sit under the shade of a tree to consume whatever it was he'd brought in his brown paper bag, while she stayed inside to eat the lunch prepared by the kitchen at the motel. From her vantage point as she ate, she looked out over the valley, where a shimmering mist was rising from the trees below.

A clear, clean, woodsy smell filled the air. The leaves falling from the huge spreading branches of the old tree near the fence were signs of the changing season, and she knew that winter was not far off. Squaring her shoulders, she headed for the kitchen and the old wood range. The black cast-iron monster dominated the tiny kitchen. After she had gathered kindling from the woodpile in back, she decided to build her first fire. She believed there could be nothing to it; all she had to do was put in some wood, strike a match and presto, she'd have a nice little blaze. Using the lifter, she removed the two round black plates from the stove, and studiously stuffed old newspapers into the fire box. Then she piled the armload of wood on top, struck a match to the paper, and quickly replaced the plates. Standing back, she briskly brushed her hands in satisfaction, believing she'd done a fine job. After a moment she turned away, planning to go out to the rain barrel, the battered old tea kettle in her hand.

The birds sang in the early morning sun as she leaned back against the house and filled the tea kettle, contentment in her expression. But as she looked back at the cabin door her eyes widened in panic. The house was on fire! Without thinking, she dashed into the smoke-filled room. Coughing and choking, she looked for the flames, but through her burning tears she saw only swiftly rising clouds of black acrid smoke coming from the stove. A lift of the front plate showed her more black malevolent smoke. Almost as if to stop her, the old stove heaved a mighty belch. Cindy was caught in a blast of thick black soot that temporarily blinded her so she had to feel her way to the door, where she stumbled as she pushed herself out into the fresh clean air. Sobbing, she panted for breath while she rubbed at her burning eyes.

Reviving, she looked toward the house, saw that the smoke was thinning, and dared to hope the fire it had blown itself out. Fresh air helped her stop coughing, but it was a long time before she was able to resist rubbing her eyes with her sooty fingers.

Charlie yelled at her from the driveway, "Miss Kelly! Miss Kelly!" From his tone, she knew she had better get around there to let him see she was all right.

"I'm okay, Charlie," she called, as she rounded the corner.

She stopped short as she saw the frightened look on Charlie's face change in rapid succession to astonishment and then to hilarity. Black soot covered her face and the only white that showed were tiny crinkled lines around her eyes.

"What's wrong with you?" she asked, as he steered her toward one of the clean windows. He whooped with laughter. When she saw her reflection in the glass, Cindy broke into giggles. She looked as if she was painted for a minstrel show.

Turning to Charlie, she explained, "That old stove is broken."

"It's not broke," Charlie stated between

chuckles. "You didn't turn the draft knob." He strode back to the kitchen and she followed. He showed her a small lever up in the pipe. "You have to turn this," he told her, "before the smoke can travel up the chimney." He flipped the knob and the smoke that was still pouring out of the stove slowly filtered down and stopped.

Cindy looked down at her black-covered body. "Well, I'll run to the creek and wash up," she said.

Charlie nodded and headed back to cutting the grass, his face wreathed in smiles.

The creek water was cold but, with the aid of soap, she was able to get the worst of the soot washed away from her face and hands. Even so, she looked forward to a hot shower in the motel room, because her hair was more black than red, and her clothes were as grimy as those of a chimney sweep. When she was once again behind the wheel of her car, she prayed no one would see her sneaking into her room.

TWO

While she was luxuriating under the hot needle spray of the shower, Cindy recalled the conversation she'd had with Charlie concerning bathing facilities at the cabin. She'd asked him, after she realized the rain barrel was her only water supply, how she was to take a bath. In his customarily terse way, Charlie told her Jenkins had used the creek as long as the weather permitted.

"But it wouldn't be private," she answered.

He looked at her as if privacy might be something she needn't worry about. "Nobody within ten miles," he said as he headed back to work. But even so, she doubted very much if she'd feel secure bathing out in the open like that, without the comfort of four walls around her. Then, too, the Indian summer wouldn't last forever. Just thinking about bathing in the icy creek in the dead of winter brought goosebumps to her flesh.

Maybe she'd get a washtub. The barrel was filled from rainwater that fell off the roof, but she could heat the water on her stove—providing she learned how to use the stove. The memory of Charlie's face as he explained about the stove brought a merry laugh to her lips as she dressed. She was sure he felt she was a babe in the woods, a city slicker who was unaware of the ways of the country. But he'd made wonderful changes in the cabin, and she was anxious to move in. If it weren't for the business with the cook stove, she'd be there right then.

When she was dressed, the telephone rang and Jan Jenkins said, "Charlie stopped by to mention that you'd almost set the house on fire, but he'd never in his life seen a girl who was as crazy about a place as you are about that cabin. Cindy, would you like to have dinner with me?"

"Oh, Jan, I'd love to," Cindy answered gratefully. "I didn't realize how much I need to talk to someone. I'm disappointed that I didn't get to stay out in the country tonight, but *tomorrow* I will."

By the next evening, a tired but very proud girl leaned against her new porch railing and listened to the evening song of the crickets and katydids. Twilight was on the land—the most beautiful hour of all. But she'd succeeded in getting herself dirty again, and she'd given up the motel room, so it was the creek or going to bed dirty. She ran through the woods with soap, towel and washcloth, knowing that darkness would fall before long.

Dreamily Cindy leaned over the bank and trailed her fingers through the slow-moving water. In the distance she could hear the babbling, upstream, as water cascaded over rocks. A dragonfly hovered above the water. Still she hesitated. But Charlie said there was no one around for miles, and she heard nothing but the sounds of the water and the buzzing insects in the grass. The silence reassured her. She pulled her shining curls to the top of her head and pinned them tight, threw another look around at the forest and down the stream, then quickly slipped out of her clothes and waded into

27

the green silent pool.

For several minutes she basked in uninhibited joy, splashing and cavorting in wild abandonment. Finally she drifted out into the middle of the deep water, closed her eyes and floated on her back. Her thick black lashes lay across creamy cheeks, and tendrils of wet curls trailed against her neck. She smiled, her full upper lip curving to reveal her small perfect teeth.

Suddenly Cindy felt a presence and abruptly opened her eyes. She looked all around in fear. A man was stretched out on the bank, his back against a tree. He was darkhaired, and he had the gall to smile at her.

"What are you doing on my land?" she began hotly.

"What are *you* doing in my fishing hole?" he countered.

"This is my land," she told him furiously. "You are trespassing, and I'll have you arrested."

His grin widened. "It's not *my* fault you decided to go skinnydipping in my favorite fishing hole, although I must admit the view is fine." He sounded cool and arrogant.

"Please get out of here," Cindy ordered between tightly clenched teeth.

His brow lifted in mocking innocence. "Leave? Why, I just got here! I'm going to have fish for my supper." Snapping open the tackle box, he took his time about fastening a fly to his hook.

"Please," Cindy cried. "I want to get out." Her teeth were chattering.

"Go right ahead," he answered in a tone of utter indifference. "You won't bother me at all." Then he indolently cast the fly into the water, uncomfortably close to her shoulder.

"You don't understand!" She motioned to the small pile of clothing at the base of the tree next to him.

"Oh, you really *are* skinnydipping!" He drew back in pretended shock.

Cindy's rage boiled over. "You clod, you fool, you get out of here or I'll set the police on you!"

"Now, now, little spitfire, keep talking like that and you'll stay in there until you turn blue," he promised. "You're beautiful when you're mad, but probably just as beautiful when your temper is not so high."

Biting back hot angry words, Cindy tossed her head, loosing the shiny red-gold curls as her green eyes flashed angrily. She didn't care if she had to stay there until morning, she'd be damned if she'd beg him to leave again. She squared her shoulders, turned her back to him and resigned herself to wait him out.

"You're behaving like a mule," he yelled, grinning. But he reeled in his line, picked up his gear and retreated silently through the lush ferns that grew along the path to the road.

Cindy's determination was wavering, because she was beginning to feel more than just a chill. I'll ask once more, nicely, she decided, then if he doesn't go away, I'll have to hold to my dignity and walk out. But she doubted that she'd ever to able to leave the sanctuary of the water, no matter how cold she became. Turning around, the pleading look on her face slowly faded as she heard a motor starting in the distance, then a crunch of tires as they rolled forward.

If I ever see that man again I'll scratch his eyes out, she promised herself. The memory of his eyes resting on her in his mocking arrogance brought a flush to her cheeks. "I will scratch his eyes out!" she muttered out loud. She hurriedly slipped into her clothes and headed up the path to the cabin, fuming all the while. In the bedroom she unpinned her curls and rubbed her hair dry. Then she took a pale-blue pants suit from her closet, determined to go to the police and have the trespasser arrested.

Driving always seemed to calm her, and by the time Cindy had reached town her temper had cooled enough for her to realize how embarrassing it would be to talk to the police, considering that she'd have to explain having been in the water with no clothes. Her face burned at the thought. She would let it go for the present, but if he ever stepped on her property again, she wouldn't be responsible for her actions, she vowed. Anyway, now that she'd cooled down a bit, she realized she couldn't bring charges against anyone if she didn't know his name. The trip into town was not entirely wasted, for Cindy had a very important purchase to make. It cheered her considerably to see Jan behind the counter in the store.

Jan's quick dark eyes missed nothing. "Why the thunderous look? Something wrong at the cabin?"

"No, everything's fine." Cindy forced a smile. "But I *do* hope you have something I need."

"And what would that be? I figured, what with the load you took out of here the last time, you had everything you could possibly need."

"I need a large tin bathtub," Cindy said grimly.

"Oh, shoot, use the creek." Jan laughed, not knowing what a sore spot she was touching on. But seeing the look that crossed Cindy's face, she sobered and spoke gently. "Of course we have bathtubs; come and I'll find you one. And while you're in town maybe we could have dinner together."

"Let's do," Cindy told her. "I've been missing some plain old girl talk."

"Fine, I'll be ready to go in about ten minutes. Would you mind waiting?"

"No," Cindy replied, "I'll just browse around until you're ready."

She stood before the pot display, trying to decide if she needed another sauce pan. Then the conversation at the lower end of the counter filtered into Cindy's consciousness and she recognized Charlie's voice.

"I hear the road survey is almost complete, then they'll start buying right of way. I hear tell they pay good money, too."

"Yes," another voice chimed in, "and for the money they pay, they could put the road straight through my house."

"You won't have to worry about spending that money, Harry," Charlie replied. "From what I hear the road won't even come *near* your house."

"Ready, Cindy?" Jan's voice startled her.

"I'm sorry," she said in a low voice. "I'm afraid you caught me eavesdropping."

"Don't worry about it," Jan assured her. "That's the talk all over town these days. Everyone's hoping the road will cross his land, although no one actually knows for sure whose land it will take."

"Why is everyone so enthusiastic over that road?" Cindy asked curiously. "I should think people would want to keep the traffic away."

"But that's just the reason they *want* the road," Jan told her earnestly. "The town needs the revenue the traffic will bring in."

"I know," Cindy sighed, "but just think of all

that peaceful unspoiled country being ruined."

"Yes, but a lot of people don't look at it the way you do. The money will bring a lot of prosperity to the town."

"Well, as long as it doesn't affect me, let's forget that dumb road and enjoy dinner, okay? We have a lot of things to talk about besides that."

Jan agreed. After they had finished dinner and she returned to her car, Cindy reminded Jan of her promise to come on her next day off to see the cabin and all the changes she'd made on it. "Try to make it soon," she called over the idling motor. "I only have a couple of weeks left of my vacation." Waving a cheerful goodby, she drove down Main Street and headed up the hill, her long, shining hair streaming behind her as she hummed softly to the music coming from the radio. She was pleased to be going home in better humor than she'd left. In the middle of her reflections, she braked hard when a dark, shadowy figure appeared out of nowhere. If she were not a skillful driver, she'd have hit the tall man who loomed suddenly under her headlights. As she brought her car to a screeching stop she raised her voice in anger. "You idiot! I could have killed you!"

"Sorry."

The voice was laconic, and belied the word. "You don't sound a bit sorry," Cindy raged.

"What the devil do you want me to do, get down on my hands and knees and beg?" A handsome face appeared at the side of the car and she recognized the mocking features of her tormentor of a few hours earlier.

"You!" She spoke icily, choosing her words with care. "I can't imagine you getting down on your hands and knees and begging. I can't even imagine your behaving in a civil way. But I *do* find it strange that you'd risk your neck by stepping out in front of a moving vehicle!"

He grinned, and light from a street lamp glistened on his teeth and in the whites of his eyes. "You were exceeding the speed limit. This is a quiet little town and in this particular spot you're only allowed to go fifteen miles an hour; you were doing at least thirty. Perhaps, I should further enlighten you by telling you my reason for stepping into your path, oh high and mighty spitfire. There's an enormous hole in the ground. I barely missed stepping into it."

"Too bad you didn't go ahead and step in it. Then maybe you'd have broken your—"

His laugh sounded loudly in the peaceful street as his hand reached in to touch the washtub she'd just purchased. "I guess that takes care of any future meetings at the old fishing hole."

Cindy made an exploding sound as she gunned the motor, too furious to trust herself to say another word. At the moment she didn't care if she ran over his big feet as she sped forward. Her cheeks burned all the way home.

When morning came Cindy put the distressing incident out of her mind, and the days at the cabin passed all too swiftly. Every moment was precious to her as she worked on her home and the grounds. As she planted tulip bulbs she was acutely aware of anticipating spring and the riot of color the flowers would bring. Already she had started clearing the weeds from the garden spot behind the house, and the next trip into town she would speak to Charlie. The first frost was but around the corner and she would need a supply of wood for the old sandstone fireplace that completely covered one wall of her small living room. Although the winters were usually mild in the southern part of the state, she wanted to be totally prepared.

Gradually she'd become accustomed to having none of the conveniences of the city and no longer thought twice about carrying her water from the cool clear spring, just as if she'd never known any other way.

Her encounter with the man at the creek, and later on the road, had put Cindy on guard. If he intended to come sulking around again she would be prepared for him, she had promised herself. But as the days passed uneventfully, she put the unpleasant encounter out of mind, realizing he was probably a stranger, down for a weekend of fishing and now long gone. Back to wherever he came from. At times, in spite of herself, the lean sardonic face appeared unbidden in her mind. She remembered the lazy gray eyes flicking over her, and a new wave of embarrassment and anger would rise in a rush.

She was working in the flowerbed, breathing in the tangy smell of the freshly turned earth, when Jan's yellow Volkswagen came up the lane. Jan scrambled out, her infectious grin lighting up her face as usual. "It's beautiful! I never thought anyone could fix up this old place. But you're worked miracles."

Hooking her thumbs into the top of her jeans, and drawing her shoulders back, Cindy said, "Yep." Her voice was a caricature of Charlie's slow drawl. "And you ain't seen nothing yet."

"Oh, Cindy," Jan said between peals of delighted laughter, "you even *looked* a little like him for a minute."

"Please," Cindy joked, "spare me the compliments. Charlie may be the best handyman in the country, but he's not much on the eyes."

"Maybe not," Jan told her between snickers, "but he sure has a crush on you."

"A crush on me?" Cindy was incredulous. "Why?"

"For heavens sake, Cindy," Jan replied. "Don't you ever look in a mirror? If I looked like you I wouldn't be stuck in this little old town. I'd go to a big town and be a model. That's what I'd do."

"You wouldn't like it," Cindy told her. "The city is too lonely."

"Lonely?" Jan snorted. "How could anyone be lonely in a big place?"

"Take my word for it," Cindy assured her, "it's more lonely than here in this small town. Come in," she invited, changing the subject. "See how different the inside of the house looks."

Jan oohed and aahed as Cindy led her through the small white-painted rooms. They sparkled in the bright sunlight that filtered through the draperies. In the bedroom Cindy had accented the white walls with indigo carpet, bedspread and draperies. A set of colorful paintings depicting the four seasons hung on the white wall.

In the living room she was pleased to hear her friend's sigh of pleasure. The huge fireplace was in the main focal point. The white sandstone had been cleaned and it glowed in the small room. The floor was scrubbed bare and the old wood had taken on a mellow shine. On shelves built along one wall were Cindy's treasures. Row after row of well-placed books, magazines and special keepsakes were displayed. On a rug in front of the fireplace, Tabby purred in quiet contentment.

Across the small couch was spread a beautiful red, blue and black patterned Navajo rug. And on the table beside the couch sat a kerosene lamp.

"Cindy, it's stunning, but I don't see how you can stand it up here with no electricity and no running water," Jan said. "Don't you miss the modern conveniences?"

"No," Cindy stated positively. "I don't miss anything from the city. I love it here and I'll never leave. Let's have lunch and then we'll explore the outside."

The girls lingered over a last cup of coffee and Jan marveled, "You sure can handle that monster." She gestured toward the old wood stove in the middle of the room. "I've lived in the country all my life and I couldn't build a fire in one of them if my life depended on it."

"We've had our differences," Cindy admitted, "but I think we'll end up friends."

"You talk as though the stove is *alive*," Jan commented.

"Well, I talk to flowers and they grow," Cindy admitted. "So why not stoves?" As she cleared the table, Jan brought the dishpan from its nail at the back door and poured hot water into it from the tea kettle.

Cindy laughed. "What did you say about conveniences? Hot water at my fingertips."

After setting things to order in the small kitchen, the girls wandered out the back door. "Hey," Jake asked, "is the old swimming hole still there?"

A dull flush passed over Cindy's face. "Yes."

"Cindy," Jan probed, "why do you get that look on your face every time I mention the creek?"

Hesitantly Cindy recounted the incident at the

36

pool. "Gosh," Jan murmured with envy. "Some people have all the luck. The way you described him he must have been one gorgeous hunk of man." Theatrically she added, "And if you let him get away."

"Let him! I would have shot him if I had a gun! Even now my blood boils when I think of that arrogant—"

"Cool your temper," Jan advised. "He's gone now anyway. Besides, he couldn't have been too bad. He seems to have made a lasting impression on you."

Shocked, Cindy turned angrily to her friend. "I most certainly was *not* impressed! He was a clod!"

"Methinks the lady doth protest too much," Jan teased. "But you know, he sounds familiar, as if I should recognize him. Oh well, if you ever see him in town, point him out to me."

"You can be sure I will," Cindy replied.

"I have a date tonight and it takes awhile for me to get beautiful. But before I go, I don't want to forget to tell you the big news. The land buyers from the road company are in town and I hear the road is coming through on this side of the valley. Now don't look so stricken. Your property will probably be missed, so you won't even know the road is there." Blithely Jan hopped into her bright yellow Volkswagen and set off down the hill, never suspecting the panic Cindy concealed.

At the cabin, she walked around aimlessly, trying to reassure herself that the news wouldn't disturb her, that there were too many other places the road could cross. But if the land buyers did come, she made up her mind to refuse to sell right-of-way; to tell them absolutely not, they'd have to go through someplace else. After all, it's still a free country, she assured herself, so they couldn't force her to sell an inch of her land.

That night was long, but just as dawn was breaking she drifted off into a restless slumber.

With early morning sunshine came a short, slightly bowlegged man who said, "Miss Kelly? I'm Ben Kindrick. I work for the McCord Construction Company and we need your land. McCord Construction will offer you a very fair price for it." He said it just as if she'd already agreed to sell out.

"But I'm not interested in selling," she told him.

"I'm araid you have no choice in the matter," he answered.

THREE

"I'm sorry, Miss Kelly," the young lawyer informed her regretfully, "but there is just no way you can win this case. You may hold them off for awhile, but they'll get a court order and eventually your place will be condemned. Your best bet is to take the offer and buy yourself a new home."

"No," Cindy answered bitterly, "if they take my place they're at least going to get a fight."

"You won't win." Arthur Corry was a new partner of the old, respectable law firm of Hinkle and Smyth. "You could get an injunction that would make them halt work on your property," he said thoughtfully, "at least until it comes to court. But you won't win. Although you might end up with more money."

"I don't care about the money," Cindy cried. "I just want to hold them off as long as possible." Drawing a ragged breath, she rose from the chair beside his desk. *"Please* help me, Mr. Corry," she said, her green eyes pleading.

Arthur Corry succumbed to the beauty of the desperate girl before him. "I'll hold them off as long as I can," he said with a sigh. "I *will* be in touch," he promised, as he gazed into her beautiful eyes.

Cindy left the lawyer's office feeling downcast, but unwilling to give up hope. The idea of huge equipment rolling into her quiet peaceful forest was upsetting. The valley would echo with the crash of trees. And all that she loved would disappear into a wide ribbon of asphalt flanked by service stations and souvenir stands. Bitterness welled up in her. It just wasn't fair. A person should not have to give up her home just because some fat rich owner of a road construction company decreed it. "Mr. McCord," she said out loud, "you might come all the way down from Louisville, but I'll be a thorn in your side for as long as I possibly can, and I'll make you pay. You might take my home but it won't come cheap." Defiance blazed from her as she made up her mind to give him a fight he wouldn't forget.

Holding her head high, stubborn determination written in every line of her body, Cindy marched down Main Street to her car. Jan's voice called her named from across the street. When Cindy ran to meet her, the dark-haired girl reached out her hands in sympathy.

"Oh, Cindy, I'm so sorry. I know how you feel. The whole town wants you to know we all like you, and even if you *do* have to leave the cabin, we'll help you find another place nearby."

"Why?" Cindy's voice was bitter. "So someone else can come along and take it too!" She knew she wasn't being fair to Jan, who had always been good to her. She had no right to take out her angry feelings on a friend.

"Jan, I didn't mean to take my misery out on you. Forgive me?" Briefly she smiled and added, "Anyway, I haven't left my little cabin yet. Oh, I know I'll eventually have to sell, but Mr. Big Shot

McCord will be sorry he ever took my place away from me. I'm not going to just hand it to him!"

"You can't fight a big company like that, Cindy," Jan protested.

"Oh, I can fight," Cindy stated positively. "I might not win, but I most assuredly can fight."

As she was about to leave the hardware store, Cindy was confronted by Charlie, who was with a couple of other men she had seen around town. Charlie surprised her by speaking what amounted to a very long speech for one who was as taciturn as he was. "You stick to your guns, Cindy. You've put a lot of work into that old place and you're about the most determined little ole gal I've ever seen in my life. Mebbe you cain't stop the road from comin' through, but by George, you can give McCord a run for his money."

"Oh, Charlie!" Cindy was close to tears as he patted her shoulder—so close that she was afraid she'd break down on the spot, which caused her to bolt for her car.

The letter arrived within three days. It was very formal and to the point. The McCord Company was distressed that Miss Kelly was dissatisfied with the offer made by them but they were sure that some reasonable agreement could be arrived at. The balance of the letter spoke of the good things the highway would bring to the community, mentioned progress, economy and a number of other things designed to mollify. But Cindy was not in the humor to be mollified. The words left her with the feeling that she'd been given a friendly pat on the head, as if she were a troublesome puppy. And the statement that Mr. McCord would arrive in town to call upon her personally struck her as an affront to her intellect, even her

41

integrity.

At last the day of the McCord visit dawned. By then Cindy had gone back to work and was commuting every day to the cabin. It had pleased her greatly to inform the McCord Company that she would not be home on the day Mr. McCord deigned to visit her; she looked on it as a delaying tactic, in spite of its being valid. But she had not dared to write to the company again to ask for a new date for the confrontation because the executive had agreed to arrive on a Saturday.

By ten o'clock in the morning tension held her body in a rigid grip as she waited for the sound of a car on the road in front of the cabin. Every few moments she retraced her steps to the living room to peer out.

Expecting a long limousine, she was surprised to see a dusty truck pull up the lane. She stood waiting expectantly on the porch, her arms folded in front of her to watch the man climb down from the truck. Suddenly the breath left her body in a gasp. "You!" she sputtered. "You! What are you doing here?" Her eyes went involuntarily to his mocking face. His dark hair glistened in the sun, and against her will she recognized the attraction that flashed through her.

He eyed her ironically. "So you're the stubborn woman who's holding up my road! I might have guessed."

"Your road?" She flushed with rage. "Well, Mr. McCord, this is my—"

"I know this is your property. It seems I've heard that before."

"Oh," she cried, her temper rising beyond control. "First a peeping tom and now a *thief.*"

Jed McCord's gray eyes glittered dangerously.

"Lady, you'd better accept the bid on your place and prepare to move. If you don't go willingly, I will personally pick you up and carry you off."

Cindy ran her fingers through her shining hair, and glared. "You dare lay a hand on me and I'll have you put in jail where you belong." Standing defiantly there on the steps in her faded jeans, her long red curls tousled, and her vivid green eyes flashing fire from between the thick black lashes, she wanted to scream and tear her hair—or his. Instead she continued to glare at him defiantly.

He brushed back his thick dark hair and roared, "You are without a doubt the most selfish woman I have ever met. Haven't you thought beyond yourself? What about the town? The people there need this road. Without it the town will dry up and blow away. Are you willing to let it happen just so you can play house?"

Cindy exploded into a ferocious rage. "You dare to call me selfish, you money grubber you! The state of the town's not worrying you," she choked. "It's your precious deadline and the money you stand to lose if you don't get the road through." Suddenly she spied the bucket of water she'd brought on the porch to water her flowers. "Get off my property," she ordered between clenched teeth. "Get off before you make me do something I'll regret."

"And what could a little thing like you do to me?" he asked mockingly.

Grabbing the bucket, she dashed the contents straight into his angry face.

"Why you—"

Whirling, she ran for the door, but he cleared the steps in two quick motions as he bounded forward, caught her arm and jerked her around. For a breathtaking moment he looked down into her wide green eyes, before he pulled her toward him. Then his lips came crashing down on hers. Stunned, she stood there trembling. She felt as though she could hardly breathe, as he ran his fingers through her long silky curls. And when he drew away his voice was gentle.

"I've wanted to do that ever since that day I saw you at the creek." He didn't see the hand that came up to crack against his jaw, but his smile was cool.

"Why, you little spitfire." His smile widened unpleasantly as he grasped her hands so she couldn't move. "Let's try that again," he said as he slowly lowered his lips to hers. She struggled against him, in spite of the almost irresistible urge to give in to his kiss, but his strong arms tightened, almost cutting off her breath, which caused her to stop fighting.

Surprised, Jed released her. Once she was free, Cindy backed away from him, hissing.

"You touch me again and I'll scratch your eyes out!" She knew her expression was like that of a cornered animal, but he didn't take another step toward her. Instead, he turned sharply, walked down the stairs and strode toward the truck. When he was behind the wheel he wasted no time in throwing it into reverse, backing up, then taking off in a roar. Not once did he look back toward the porch where Cindy stood, unmindful of the tears that spilled down her cheeks.

Cindy watched the truck disappear into the distance, and her shoulders sagged in defeat. Slowly she brushed the tears from her cheeks and wandered down the porch steps to smooth the dirt in the tulip bed that she had so happily planted just a few days before. Cindy had to admit to herself that Jed McCord was right: she was being selfish. The town did need and want the road. So when Ben Kindrick came to talk to her one last time a few days later, he was surprised to find the defiant tigress had lost her spirit.

She stood and gazed out over the valley and he noticed how the slim shoulders sagged in defeat. When she turned and said, "I know why you're here, Mr. Kindrick," her voice quivered.

"Miss Kelly," he began persuasively, "I have to make you see—"

"You can save your breath, Mr. Kindrick," she said, halting him in mid-argument. "I've decided to accept your offer. I won't stand in your way any longer." She turned away from him and stared blindly into the distance. She seemed to draw on an inner strength as she straightened her back and asked, "How will it be before I have to leave?"

"Well, now, Miss Kelly," he said, trying to hide the elation in his voice. "With our work schedule and what has to be done before we can start here, I think I can safely promise a month. I hope in the meantime you will find a place you'll love at much as this one."

"I don't think that will happen. I wouldn't want to take a chance on another home. Besides, there is no other like this."

Ben couldn't help but ask as he prepared to leave, "What made you change your mind, Miss Kelly?"

Stoically she stared over his shoulder. "I don't know, Mr. Kindrick," she said softly. "I guess I just got tired of fighting."

Cindy watched Ben's truck disappear down the lane and in a way she felt relieved. Deep within herself she knew she had done the right thing.

FOUR

Cindy spent the next few days alone. She walked through the forest, scuffling the bright autumn leaves beneath her feet. She decided to enjoy the month she had. She wouldn't go back to the city. That would mean her job, but now she could afford to stay and spend her time here. Perhaps later she could find a job in this town. Cindy liked the people here and they seemed to like her; maybe she would stay after all. She would go down and talk to Jan about it. Belatedly she remembered the young lawyer and realized she would have to go to town that very afternoon. He was probably working on her case right now. She hated to tell him that she'd backed down, but she knew he had to be told before he wasted any more time on the case. Cindy turned back to the house and hurriedly dressed for the trip to town.

A short time later, clad in a white linen pant suit, looking cool and assured, her long red-gold hair twisted on top of her head, Cindy slid into the seat of the car, perched large sunglasses on her small pert nose, and drove with competent skill down the narrow lane.

She drove into town and parked in front of the hardware store. She paused in the doorway to call to Jan, "How about lunch?"

Jan looked up and pleasure shone on her face. "Sure. Meet you at the diner at noon, okay?" At Cindy's nod, she turned her attention back to the customer waiting patiently at the counter.

"Nice lady," Cindy heard him say as she left the store.

She was met at the door of the office by a thoroughly delighted young lawyer. Although he had not made much progress in her case, he was happy to see her again. Solicitously he led her to the chair beside his desk. As he sat opposite her he stared at her beautiful troubled face.

"What's wrong?" he asked, his brown eyes worried.

"Oh, Mr. Corry, I've signed a deal with the road company, and I want you to stop all proceedings against them."

"Well, I think you did the right thing." Arthur Corry seemed relieved. "But you were so determined; why did you change your mind?"

At the question this time Cindy answered truthfully, "I realized what the road meant to the town," she said, a resigned look on her face. "I knew I had only been thinking of myself. The people here need this road and I won't fight it at the expense of my friends."

"You're a very unselfish and understanding person, Miss Kelly. I don't think your friends here can fully appreciate what you're giving up for them."

"Everyone has been so nice to me here, I couldn't hurt them. Besides," she stated with a little more life in her voice, "I intend to stay in Pine Valley and watch it grow."

"Good," he exclaimed, pleasure in his voice. "I

47

must say you'll be a beautiful addition to the town. To celebrate, will you have dinner with me tonight?"

Smiling at him, she nodded. "I'd love to, Mr. Corry."

"Call me Arthur; I think we're friends."

"Call me Cindy," she laughingly agreed. "I know we're friends."

He walked her to the door. As she crossed the street he called after her, "Pick you up at seven," which Cindy acknowledged with a wave.

She crossed the street to the diner. As she entered she saw Jan waving from a booth in the rear.

"I hope you're hungry," she said to Cindy. "I'm starved!"

"Oh, Jan, you're always starved."

"Yes, I know." Jan glanced ruefully down at her plump figure and then she grinned. "One of these days I'm going on a diet. I don't know when, but I will!"

They ordered lunch. Over her toasted cheese Cindy filled Jan in on the events of the past few days. "And I've decided to stay in Pine Valley," she said.

"Oh, Cindy, I'm so glad! I was afraid that after you lost your place you wouldn't want to stay here. I'd have really missed you."

"Well, now all I have to do is ind a place to stay."

"That's simple," Jan broke in. "There's a room for rent down at my boarding house."

"No." Cindy spoke slowly. "I'd really like a small house; I want more than just one room. I like to cook and I want my own kitchen. Hey!" she exclaimed, "why don't you come in with me; we'll go shares on a house?"

At first Jan's eyes glowed, but the excitement slowly faded. "I don't think I can afford it. It would take a lot of money to buy a house."

"Why buy? We can rent, can't we?"

"Well," Jan said slowly, the glow returning to her eyes, "I guess we could. By gosh, I know we could." Now she was as excited as Cindy. "I'll be off Saturday. Do you want to start looking then?"

"Yes, we'll start looking Saturday!"

Incredibly Cindy's spirits, which had been so low before, were soaring. As she drove home she recounted the events of the day. She had a new roommate, tomorrow they'd look for a new home, and last of all, she had a date for dinner with a rising young lawyer.

Suddenly she remembered Brent, and guilt assailed her. She realized she hadn't thought of him in days. Although he had tried to meet her after she returned to her job in Lexington, she had always managed to put him off. Now she knew she couldn't dodge the issue any longer. She had to make a decision; then both of them could go on with their lives.

Although she still had feelings for Brent, she knew they could never make it together. The pain and heartache were a lesson well taught. Never again would she take a good-looking man at face value.

Now a man like Arthur, she told herself, was ideal—kind, gentle and quiet, a man who represented security, solidity and no danger of being hurt. Here was someone she could be comfortable with and there would be no ties on either of them. Arthur was interested in her, Cindy knew, and maybe that was what she needed at this time.

Cindy resolved to meet with Brent as soon as

possible to return his ring. But as she entered the lane and saw the little cabin nestled among the trees, she felt its loss deep within her.

She shrugged off her sad feelings and decided to quit feeling sorry for herself. She spent the remaining hours of the afternoon carrying water from the old rain barrel to the shiny new tub sitting in the middle of the kitchen floor. She added hot water from the tea kettle she kept on the old range. The warm soapy water caressed her creamy skin as she settled her neck against the back of the tub. Languidly she raised one slender leg and washed her small foot.

Cindy's bath had put her in a relaxed mood and she was looking forward to dinner with Arthur. As she donned her lacy underwear, she decided to rest awhile for the evening ahead. She lay down across the bed and quickly drifted off to sleep.

She awoke to see shadows lengthening across the window. As she lay there in the cool breeze, she heard a car pull into the lane. She jumped to her feet and glanced at the clock. *It was seven.* Hurriedly she slipped into a pale green sundress with tiny straps, and slid white sandals on her small feet. She ran to the mirror, pulled her hair up away from her face and fastened it on top, allowing it to cascade in long curling strands to her shoulders. Then she pulled a few shining tendrils loose around her face. As the car stopped in front of the house, she added a touch of pale lipstick, a dash of cologne and she was ready to go.

Cindy stepped out on the porch just as Arthur turned from the car. Smiling, she ran lightly down the steps. Arthur's eyes widened; removing his thick glasses, he swallowed. He had never seen a girl more lovely!

"Hi," she said, as he opened the car door for her.

He smiled down at her. "Cindy, you're very beautiful." Suddenly waves of red suffused his face. The unflappable Arthur Corry, who was never at a loss for words in the courtroom, was speechless. "I'm as nervous as a schoolboy," he said.

Cindy was touched by his admission. "Oh, Arthur, why should you be nervous?"

"Well, I've never had a date with someone as beautiful as you," he said seriously.

"Flatterer." She smiled. "Let's go eat, I'm starved!"

Arthur was grinning as he closed the door for her and trotted around the car. "Do you like to dance?" he asked as he settled under the wheel.

"Oh, yes," she glowed happily. "I love to dance, although it's been awhile since I did it. Is there a place in Pine Valley?"

"No, we're going to Bradford tonight, unless you want to eat at the diner," he said seriously.

Cindy laughed, her green eyes sparkling. "Oh, no, Bradford will be fine!"

Her amusement was infectious and Arthur smiled over at her. "The food at the diner could stand improvement," he admitted.

Arthur drove with care and, as he concentrated on the road ahead, the conversation trailed off into silence. But it was a comfortable quiet. Cindy relaxed and enjoyed the ride.

He wasn't exciting, she mused, but he was restful and she liked his quiet company. At the moment she didn't want or need anything more. Glancing over at Arthur as he peered owlishly at the road ahead, Cindy mentally compared him to Brent. She knew there wasn't any danger of being hurt by him. Before she knew it, he had parked the car and they were dashing across a busy street to the Club Graystone.

They entered the club and were quickly seated in an intimate, shadowy corner. The hostess had mistaken them for lovers. Arthur seemed pleased by this and made no move to correct the idea. He had noticed the admiring glances Cindy received from the many male customers, and she was amused to see him swell perceptibly.

Cindy leaned back and sighed. His company was soothing and the food was wonderful. She sipped her wine and longingly watched the dancers. Arthur noted this and, catching hold of her hand, he pulled her up. "Let's dance." Cindy decided to enjoy the dance. Smiling at him, she closed her eyes, leaned her head against his shoulder and lost herself in the slow dreamy waltz.

Suddenly she heard a familiar voice from the table beside the dance floor. "Well, our little spitfire seems to be recovering nicely," she heard Ben Kindrick remark to Jed McCord, as he threaded his way to a small table from the dance floor with a girl on his arm.

"Why?" Jed asked, looking away from the girl at the next table who was flirting with him. "Where did you see her?" Without a word, Ben pointed over his shoulder at the dance floor. Jed's gaze followed his finger, and she saw his gray eyes narrow. Her long red hair gleamed in the dim light as Cindy swayed dreamily and listened to the two men discussing her. As she danced she watched them through lowered lashes.

Jed's lips tightened. "She doesn't seem to be in too bad shape."

"A bad shape she will never be in," Ben quipped.

With that he turned back to the giggling girl beside him.

Abruptly, Jed excused himself, his eyes hard. He left the table and headed toward the dance floor. Cindy tried not to open her eyes as she saw him coming toward them. But she finally had to look up into his hard gray eyes. Dressed in a dark denim suit, a lock of dark hair falling across his forehead, he was forebodingly handsome.

"Hello," he said to Arthur. "May I cut in?" Arthur was flustered, but he nodded. Jed smiled in dark amusement at her escort and Cindy smoldered in silent resentment. How she hated the thought of having to be civil to *him* while they danced.

Stiffly she allowed Jed to pull her into his embrace. "Control your temper, Spitfire." His low voice held a hint of amusement. Ruthlessly he pulled her unyielding body to his. "Relax," he taunted, his lips against her ear. "You seemed to enjoy dancing awhile ago."

"And you seem to enjoy baiting me." She was trembling with rage. "What do you want from me?" Her voice quivered as strange feelings surged through her—feelings she didn't want, feelings she fought against.

Suddenly he stopped dancing and stared down at her. Her wide eyes grew frightened as she looked into his grim face. "I'll be damned if I know," he said. Although his voice had been harsh, his touch was gentle as they finished the dance in silence.

He left her at the table, gave Arthur a curt nod and strode away without looking back.

FIVE

Restlessly, Cindy leaned against the porch railing and listened as all the little creatures of the night sang to her from the dark shadows of the yard. A lonely owl hooted from the blackness of the dense forest, and the wind ruffled the dry autumn leaves still clinging to the trees, making them whisper. High overhead, the bright September moon traced a silver path from the cabin to the sleeping valley below. Way down at the end of her drive she could see the flash of lights in the trees as Arthur's big car pulled onto the highway and headed back down the hill toward Pine Valley. Perturbed, she listened as the steady drone of the motor faded into the distance. She was alone in the stillness of the night.

She was lonely for the first time since leaving the city. Discontented and restless, she wandered over to the steps and sat down, wondering why she felt so depressed and moody. The quiet of the country had always soothed her troubled spirits, but tonight the silence intensified her feeling of aloneness.

Resting her chin on the palms of her hands, she gazed out over the shadowy hills and shivered in the cool night wind. Abruptly, her mind returned to the night club. Her date had started on an easy note. Arthur's relaxed companionship had made the evening comfortable and fun, for it had been a long time since she'd gone out with anyone but Brent. The elegant atmosphere of the night club, combined with Arthur's patent admiration, had chased all thoughts of Brent from her mind and she felt as though she'd been freed from a cage. She remembered passing a mirror and seeing her face, radiant and sparkling. Her long copper hair had caught the soft light and glowed. With every sweep of thick lashes, contentment was reflected in her emerald eyes. She'd enjoyed the club, the food had been great, and the dancing heavenly.

At least it had been until that arrogant, miserable excuse for a man, Jed McCord, showed up!

Cindy shifted uneasily on the step and her face flamed hotly as she remembered the intimate way he'd held her as they danced. She could still feel the heat of his hard lean body and the roughness of his denim jacket against her cheek. The musky smell of his aftershave assailed her senses and the tight grip of his arms cut off her breath as she stubbornly gritted her teeth and fought the surge of dizziness in her head.

His lazy gray eyes held amusement as he'd noted her studied indifference when they moved gracefully around the floor. Breathlessly she'd glared at his evident relish of her discomfort— although now that she was safely away from him she did admit to a moment of fright when he stopped dancing and stared into her eyes. It irritated her to recall how she trembled within his grasp while primitive feelings chased the contentment from her. It was as though McCord had set out to ruin the evening for her, and he had. "He deliberately ruined everything," she fumed aloud in the darkness.

Jed had left the club immediately following their dance, but he'd cast a pall upon the night and Cindy hadn't been able to regain her easy mood no matter how hard she tried.

Stoically Arthur had ignored her bad humor, but it was an embarrassingly long time before she'd been able to carry her end of the conversation. The brightness of the club had faded and she'd been relieved when Arthur finally suggested they start for home.

Poor Arthur. Of course he'd noticed the effect Jed McCord had on her. The man made her blood boil! Arthur would have to be blind not to notice, but good manners prevented his mentioning it.

Cindy was jolted from her reverie as a dark shadow swooped from a tall tree beside the house. On widespread wings it flew like an arrow toward the barn. A high thin squeal pierced the stillness of the night, then all was quiet . . . . The owl had found its prey.

She stood in the dark confines of the porch and shivered at the ruthless cruelty of nature. Suddenly living alone in the country wasn't as thrilling as it had been. She was beginning to think solitude was fine . . . up to a point!

Without a backward glance, Cindy slipped into the house and fumbled for the lamp. A wooden match flared in the velvet darkness of the room and she welcomed the small flame as it chased the shadows to far corners and brought Tabby tripping on light paws to greet her.

With the lamp held high in her hand, the cat padding behind, Cindy entered the bedroom. She set the small flickering source of light on the table beside the bed and restlessly began to lay out her night clothes.

As her unsettled feelings surfaced once again, she tried to ignore the invariable return of the thoughts that had haunted her before. She slipped the sandals from her feet and reached up to loosen the shining copper curls, allowing them to cascade over her shoulders. She shrugged from her clothes and wandered over to the mirror.

With pensive green eyes she regarded the reflection in the glass. The flickering flame of the lamp caressed her creamy skin in a warm rosy glow. Sensuously her fingers lightly traced gentle curves as she stood watching the girl in the mirror. It was as though she were watching a stranger, and she couldn't understand what was causing her to feel so dismal.

Conflicting emotions suffused her mind and her stomach lurched as a dark handsome face with flinty gray eyes intruded upon her thoughts. She forced the picture to fade, angry with herself for allowing it to come, but she was baffled by the deep, unsated yearning that welled from within.

Briskly she plumped the pillow and climbed into bed. She lay beneath the white sheets and willed sleep to come, but the first gray light of dawn was showing beneath the windowshade before she settled into a deep, dreamless slumber.

She felt as though she'd just closed her eyes when the alarm shattered the silence of the room. Groggily she fumbled for the noisy little box, upsetting it from the table, where it fell to the floor and proceeded to turn in wild circles as it clamored for her to get up. Her long slender arm came from under the blanket and she groped around the floor for the clock. But in an instant the alarm ran down and, with a few slow tings, the racket stopped. She burrowed under the covers and slipped into a light doze.

Her green eyes snapped open as she remembered she had made plans with Jan to look for a house. Dangling her feet sideways over the bed, she hunted for the clock that just a few minutes before had been such a nuisance. Eight o'clock! She was supposed to meet Jan at nine-thirty! Yawning, she pushed her still weary body from the bed and headed for the kitchen to get the fire going. It was days like this that she most missed the easy convenience of indoor plumbing and electricity.

It was a cool crisp September morning but the sun shining through the bright autumn leaves promised another day of Indian summer. A little brown bird sang merrily from the old apple tree by the back door; it didn't seem to mind the breeze the ruffled the leaves around it.

"Hush," Cindy scolded as she bent over the rain barrel and filled the battered tea kettle left by the previous owner of the cabin. "Some of us didn't sleep as well as you did last night."

Cindy wasn't in a cheerful frame of mind. The long restless night had taken its toll, as the dark shadows beneath her green eyes and sooty lashes demonstrated.

She let the screen door bang behind her as she carried the tea kettle over and placed it on the back plate of the huge black stove. It seemed to take forever for the aroma of freshly perked coffee to fill the room and she poured a steaming cup, hoping the hot beverage would bolster her low spirits and stimulate some interest in the forthcoming day.

Wearily she carried her coffee over to the small table and sank into a chair. She brushed tousled curls from her face as her troubled eyes traveled around the room. The bright wallpaper and ruffled curtains were reflections of the happy ideas she'd had for the small kitchen just a short time before, but now all her plans had to be laid to rest. In just a matter of days the little house would be gone.

She smiled as she recalled the day the old stove drenched her with the thick black soot, and Charlie's mirth at the sight of her black face. Her antics had brought smiles to the faces of the townspeople as she'd tried to make her way in the country, but they'd expressed admiration at her grit and it made her proud to know they wanted her to stay in Pine Valley. Okay, she would lose the farm but she still had her new friends and the enjoyment of living in the country as she had always dreamed.

Thoughts of her new friends made her glance down at the watch on her wrist. A few more minutes of woolgathering and she would be late meeting Jan! As soon as she had gulped the last of her coffee, she dashed to the bedroom to change and brush her hair. A few minutes later she was driving down the highway to town.

Cindy's dark shadowed eyes were hidden behind the rosy lens of her large sunglasses as she pulled the small car over to the curb and parked in front of Jan's boarding house. Since she was right on time she expected Jan to appear, but after several minutes had passed, she realized Jan probably hadn't seen her drive up.

As she got out of the car, a disembodied voice

whispered loudly from the tall green hedge next to the drive, "Pst! Pst! I'm coming, so don't get out!"

Cindy couldn't believe her eyes as Jan darted from the bushes and jumped into the small car.

"Drive," Jan ordered, watching the house intently.

Startled, Cindy complied, her tires protesting loudly as she pulled from the curb and roared down the street. The scene reminded her of bank robbery sequences in B movies and she felt as if she were driving the getaway car.

As they reached the corner, Jan turned around in her seat and breathed a big sigh of relief. "You can slow down now!" She grinned, her brown eyes sparkling mischievously.

"What's going on?" Cindy asked, as she slowed the car and shot a confused look at her friend.

"My landlord is Skeeter Bain," Jan replied, as though that should answer all Cindy's questions.

"So who's Skeeter Bain?" Cindy darted a questioning glance at Jan as she halted at the stop sign on Main Street.

"I know you've met Skeeter. He owns the motel too. You must have talked to him when you stayed there. Remember how hard it was to get away from him? Well, I hate to say it, but when he's home I sneak out. That way I can get where I'm going on time."

"I remember," Cindy laughed ruefully. "I sneaked out a few times too. I figured he was probably lonesome."

"Lonesome, ha! He has a wife and she's as bad as he is! They're just plain nosey! Everything Skeeter hears goes home to Louise and from Louise it goes to the Wednesday afternoon garden club and from there on everyone in town knows all about it."

"Oh, Jan, surely you exaggerate!" Cindy grinned.

"You think so, do you? Listen to this; you went out with Arthur Corry last night; you went dancing at the Graystone, and you saw Jed McCord too." Lifting her head, Jan pointed to the right. "Go down highway fifty. Maggy Jenson has a place for rent."

Cindy was flabbergasted. Raising her sunglasses from her nose, she gaped at Jan. "How did you know we went to Bradford? That's thirty miles from Pine Valley."

"Haven't you heard the old saying, everyone knows everyone else's business in a small town? Well, it's true. Doubly so with you because the people can't figure you out. You're young, beautiful, and now that you've sold your farm you have money. Everyone wonders why you're staying in the valley."

"I love the country, Jan. I have no ulterior motives! I want to live as my grandmother did and I'm going to. The people here are friendly and trustworthy. Some of them don't even lock their doors. You sure couldn't do that in the city."

"Gosh, Cindy, I know how you feel about the country," Jan said. "The Lord knows I've heard you rave often enough about how wonderful it is to live down here, but I think you're looking at it through rose-colored glasses. People here are human too. We have our bad ones and our good ones just like the city."

"I suppose," Cindy replied, as she skillfully maneuvered the small car around a twisting curve in the road, "but I've met a lot of people and none have been anything but friendly and helpful. So you surely don't have too many bad ones."

"Maybe not." Jan shrugged, and then she grinned widely. "But I bet we have more gossips!"

"They're not gossips, Jan. They're just curious."

Jan giggled as she remembered something she'd heard down at the hardware store. "Guess who Sudie Perice thinks you are? Ann-Margaret, hiding from her public."

"You be sure and thank Sudie for keeping my secret for me," Cindy said, laughing.

"Have you met Sudie and Millie yet?" Jan asked, amused.

"No, I haven't, but I'd like to. I'm sure I'd like Sudie." Cindy smiled.

"Yes, I believe you'd like them both," Jan said thoughtfully.

"Everyone in town knows Sudie Perice and Millie Corry."

"Millie Corry?" Cindy asked at the familiar name.

"Yep, that's right. Millie is Arthur's mother. She and Sudie are best friends and have been for over fifty years. They quarrel constantly but I think that's why they enjoy each other's company so much. It adds spice to their lives." Abruptly, Jan pointed toward a lane as they drove past it. "We should have turned in there."

"Jan, you could give me a little more notice," Cindy said reprovingly as she brought the car to a halt, put it into reverse and backed up to the narrow road. Carefully she drove down a short lane and parked in front of a tidy white house with black shutters. A tall weeping willow shaded the edge of the porch, where a rose arbor held the remnants of a few late blooms. The picturesque farmhouse was very appealing.

"Isn't it pretty?" Jan exclaimed as they sat in the car. "It's the kind of place that would be ideal as a honeymoon cottage."

"Maybe for you, but I don't think I'll ever have a need for a place to spent a honeymoon!" Cindy's mouth held a slightly bitter taste as she slid abruptly from the car and walked to the house, with Jan following.

As she passed the roses, she stopped and picked one of bright pink blossoms. A strong sweet smell permeated the air, but even as she held the rose petals fell to the ground like snowflakes. Suddenly she was holding only a memory in her hand. The rose was gone and in its place she held a bare branch with thorns.

"Cindy?" Jan spoke quietly, aware of the forlorn look Cindy had as she looked at the long thorny switch. "You're holding back secrets. Sometimes it helps to talk about things that bother you. I'm your friend and I want to help if I can."

Cindy's eyes were bleak as she turned to Jan and saw the earnest concern on her face.

"Everyone in town is wondering why I moved down here and some, like Sudie Perice, have drawn their own conclusions. The truth is, I came to get away from a man." The confession came slowly, and with effort, but once it was out she was glad she had spoken.

Jan nodded slowly, her suspicions confirmed. "I thought so," she said, a sad empathy in her wide brown eyes.

"See this?" Cindy's voice was bitter as she held out the bare ugly stem that moments ago had held the limp petals of a once beautiful rose. "Love goes in cycles too. It blooms as fresh and bright as a flower in the spring, and just as you think it will

63

last forever something happens that's as damaging as a killing frost. Before you know it, faith, trust and happiness drop like petals in the wind and your heart is as bare as this stick."

"You've been hurt, Cindy, but don't let yourself be as bitter as you sound. All men aren't bad. You've just had one painful experience," Jan said. "I know it sounds crazy now, but later on you may be glad this happened. Someone may come along who was meant for you."

"Oh, Jan," Cindy sighed, "I don't think I'll ever trust a man again." Hesitantly she talked of Brent and the terrible pain and loneliness that had brought her to Pine Valley. "Loving someone leaves you vulnerable, and I don't want to be hurt again!"

"I knew you'd removed a ring when I saw that pale spot on your finger," Jan said sympathetically. "But Cindy, you can't hide from life or love forever. Go see Brent and maybe you'll be able to lay all these hurt feelings to rest. You're still tied to him by hurt as much as you were before by love. See him again and set yourself free."

Cindy walked over to the porch step and sat down, still holding the flowerless stem. "I know, I've told myself that too," she admitted. "And I will. It's time we were both free."

"Good. Now hang on to that thought," Jan said, as she pulled open the door of the house and peered inside. "Come on, let's look it over. If working on one house helped you before, maybe it'll be even more therapeutic this time. The walls need to be papered, but other than that this house seems to be in pretty good shape. Oh, Cindy," she added, as Cindy walked into the room. "I hate to be the bearer of bad news, but this place has a bathroom and electricity! You may be all country and enjoy the back-to-nature trip, but I like modern conveniences."

Jan's efforts to cheer her up had not gone unnoticed and, realizing what a great friend she had found, Cindy resolved to be more cheerful. "I guess I could put up with some of these modern contraptions," she replied with an exaggerated drawl. "If you like the house, we'll rent it."

"I love it!" Jan bubbled. "But do you?"

"Well . . . it's not the cabin, but it has its own charm and I think it will be fine." Suddenly curious, Cindy turned to Jan. "What about Hank? How does he feel about our sharing a place? After all, you *are* engaged."

Jan cocked her head to one side, her funny little face serious, her brown eyes wide. "You've heard of long engagements? Well, mine will probably be the longest on record. Hank loves me, I know. But he's afraid of responsibility and he has no confidence in himself. Frankly, I think he's delighted we're going to share a place because that way he doesn't have to make a decision for awhile longer."

Although Jan was trying to be flip as she spoke, Cindy sensed a deep hurt. She doubted if Jan would ever admit it, but she detected a hint of fear that Hank would never set a date for their marriage.

"It seems we both have man troubles, but we'll work them out. Don't worry, Hank will come to his senses. He'd be a fool not to! You're a great girl, Jan. He'll pop the question, just you wait and see."

"Do you really think so?" Jan's countenance brightened considerably as she gazed hopefully at

Cindy.

"Sure I do!" Cindy replied firmly. "All men get cold feet before setting the date. Now come on, let's quit feeling sorry for ourselves and look this place over. That is, if we intend to live here."

Both girls were a little self-conscious after telling their innermost secrets, but they now shared a closeess that hadn't been there before, and each in her own way felt a sense of relief at having unburdened herself.

Cindy was glad she'd finally been able to talk about Brent. Just the telling had helped. Keeping all the hurt inside had made it worse, and for some time thoughts of him had colored her moods and caused her to be short tempered. Jan was right: she would have to see Brent and finish it once and for all.

Hours later, two tired but pleased girls parted company. The paperwork was completed and signed all around. Now they could begin the work of making the house livable. With big plans for the following weekend, Cindy waved to goodby to Jan at the boarding house and drove out of town for home.

As she turned into the drive from the highway, exhaustion washed over her and she was almost ready to cry with relief at being able to park the car in the barn. The long sleepless hours of the night before were catching up with her and fatigue had come down suddenly. She was so weary she closed her eyes and leaned back against the warm seat, too tired to move for a second.

Far in the west, she could hear a low rumbling, a warning that a thunderstorm was in the offing. The closed mustiness of the dark shadowy barn was warm and peaceful and Cindy couldn't seem to find the energy to climb from the car to go to the house. High overhead in the rafters, fat pigeons fluttered uneasily at the approaching bad weather.

The wind had risen; she could hear it whistling through the trees outside. The shadows in the building had deepened preceptibly when she opened her lashes and peered around. Raindrops plopped sotly on the tin roof above her. She realized she'd better start for the house, because the storm was going to be worse than she had first imagined. As she started toward the big double doors, a bright shaft of silver lightning lit up the sky and the building shook as the ensuing boom crashed violently, echoing awesomely across the valley below.

Stunned, Cindy stood in the open doors and watched as a heavy wall of rain moved across the hills. It would soon be upon the farm, and her frightened senses told her to run to the house. But even as she hesitated, the rain pounded the roof in a raging torrent. Shaking with fear, she knew she'd have to brave the weather in the ramshackle old building. The wind renewed its assault on the trees outside and she wondered if the old barn could hold up under the violence of the storm.

Fear overwhelmed her as she was almost blinded by a bolt of lightning that hit the rusty wire fence beside the rutted road and sizzled across it. Turning away, Cindy clasped her trembling hands to her cheeks and struggled to hold on to her composure.

Without warning, she was grasped by the arm and pushed firmly away from the open doors. A blind panic overwhelmed her as she fought against strong sinewy arms that held her.

"Stop it, you little fool!" Jed's dark angry face came into focus as he shook her violently. "Did you want to be struck by lightning?"

Trembling, she collapsed against his broad chest while his strong arms enfolded her. It was pure instinct that caused her to burrow closer in the safety of his embrace. Moments later she realized what she was doing and opened wide tear-stained eyes to ask with a gulp, "What . . . what are you doing here?"

Suddenly the building shook as the boom of thunder rolled across the hill, and Cindy trembled in terror.

Jed's gray eyes grew dark as he absently ran his fingers through the long red curls that lay on her shoulder. "You surprise me, Spitfire," he murmured as he bent and gently kissed the corners of her wet eyes. "I didn't think anything could frighten you." Then, with a ragged oath, he crushed her in his arms and parted her quivering red lips with a searing kiss.

Involuntarily Cindy's arms crept around his neck as she swayed against him and welcomed his embrace. A slow warmth flickered to life in the pit of her stomach and her senses reeled as he kissed the fluttering pulse in the hollow of her throat.

As the storm raged outside the door, Cindy succumbed to the one in her soul. His mouth returned to her parted lips and his hands stroked the warmth into a flame. She reeled from the impact of his masculinity as his hand slipped under her shirt and caressed the satiny swell beneath.

Deep within the recesses of her mind she was shocked by her wanton behavior, but at the same time she breathlessly ached to feel him next to her bare body. She had to stop him now, knowing that if she hesitated for even a moment she would be lost. Furiously she fought the raising tide of emotions that threatened to engulf her. Clenching her small hands into fists, she wrenched herself from his arms.

"Do you grab every woman you meet?" She ground the words out through her painfully tightened throat. "You seem to think you can grab *me* every chance you get!"

"Oh, hell!" The expletive reflected Jed's feelings as he glared at her. "You were the one who grabbed!"

"I was frightened! I would have held on to anyone. You took advantage of my fear! Are you so desperate for a woman that you use *fear* to get what you want?" Cindy's lip curled with contempt.

"I have all the women I need. I'm not so desperate that I'd come chasing after a stubborn, silly little redhead who's never grown up. I like *women*, not little girls!" Jed's tone was as contemptuous as Cindy's.

"It sounds as if you've never settled down with one woman in your life. I pity the poor girl who gets you!" Cindy cried scornfully.

"I don't intend to be *got*, as you put it, Spitfire," Jed said coldly. "The women I like are realistic. They enjoy momentary pleasures the same as I do, and they don't tease and then use their virtue as a shield the way you do, either."

Stung by his accusation, Cindy gritted her teeth and asked, "What are you doing here anyway?"

Jed turned away and walked to the barn door. Silently he watched the raging storm outside. He didn't act as if he were going to answer her question.

Cindy stared at his broad shoulders and her anger increased. "I asked what you wanted here!"

"I came to see if you needed help moving, but with your temper, I don't think the offer would be appreciated," Jed said mildly, but his eyes still held a smoldering anger.

"If I needed help, Mr. McCord," she told him coldly, turning away to hide her shakiness, "I wouldn't ask you! Anyway, my time isn't up yet, so don't be in such a big hurry to tear up my farm."

"I'm not worried about this place. It'll be here when I get ready to work on it," Jed drawled.

"And you'll love it, won't you?" Cindy's eyes shot fire. "Does it ever keep you awake at night, Mr. McCord, thinking about the people whose homes you've stolen?"

"I don't steal places, Miss Kelly. I buy them, and for a nice price, I might add." Jed's jaw jutted dangerously and his voice grated. "You should know! I paid enough for this pile of rocks. You're just being stubborn. A spoiled little city girl like you doesn't really care about a place like this. You're probably bored as hell, but you wouldn't admit it, would you?"

"You seem to think you know all about me," Cindy said with deceptive calm, but her green eyes blazed with scorn as she watched him walk toward her across the dusty floor.

He towered over her and she could see the anger that burned in his gray eyes. "I've met brats like you before," he said, his words filled with disgust. "This was your little playhouse in the country and that's all it was. Why don't you grow up?"

Cindy wanted to hit him; the urge was so strong that she had to clench her hands behind her back and hold her furious temper in check. She wondered what he would do if she did strike him. The answer to that question flashed into her mind immediately. He would return the blow without hesitation!

"You have no right to determine my motives for wanting to live down here." Her voice shook with suppressed rage. "I love this place and I wouldn't *ever* have grown tired of it!" But even as she vehemently denied his accusation, a nagging doubt entered her mind.

The loneliness and restlessness of the night before haunted her. Was he right? Was she losing interest in the little place? But as these doubts whirled through her head, anger spurred her on. "You are contemptible! You just wish I were tired of it," she cried. "That would ease your conscience, wouldn't it?"

"Damn it, look at yourself. You're worn out! Between this place and driving back and forth to Lexington, you're killing yourself! Why do you keep hanging on? You're a hothouse rose, Spitfire, and you don't have the stamina to keep it up." Jed's sarcastic tone cut into her like a knife.

"You take care of your business and let me tend to mine," she retorted. *"I'll leave when the month is up, and not until.* Now you get off my property!"

"My property, if you don't mind," he taunted with derision. "This place belongs to me. If you're not prepared to leave then I might decide to stay until you do."

"You wouldn't care," Cindy whispered as she retreated under his glare. "And you can't scare me with empty threats, either!"

"No?" he jeered. "Who said it was an empty threat? And what would you do if I did stay? Send your boyfriend after me?"

Shocked, Cindy stared at him in confusion, wondering how he knew about Brent.

"Of course, with him being a lawyer, you might have a chance of getting me out. Would you like to take a chance on it?" Jed grinned at her.

She realized he was talking about Arthur; he thought they were serious about one another. Well, she would just let him go on thinking it. If he thought a lawyer was behind her, he'd watch what he said and did.

"He's a better man than you, and he will have something done if I ask him to!" She flung the words at him angrily as she crossed her fingers behind her back, hoping Arthur would forgive her this little white lie. "Now get out of here and don't come back until I'm gone!"

Turning on her heel, she dashed from the barn through the driving rain, to the house.

SIX

A strong gusty wind blew soggy leaves across the asphalt highway, mute reminders of Saturday's violent storm. But Cindy didn't notice as she drove toward Lexington that Monday morning. Her mind was on the problems ahead.

She would hand in her two-week notice, see Brent and return his ring. Cindy didn't know which job she dreaded most. Mr. Ames would panic and she hated to leave him, after he'd praised her so heartily and been so kind.

She had no idea how Brent would react to the news. He'd made it clear that he wanted a reconciliation, but it would never work. He wasn't the kind of man to settle down with one woman. Jan had been right and she had known it all along, although she hadn't been willing to face it. So now she would set him free.

Suddenly Brent's face faded from her mind, to be replaced by a dark sardonic vision of the angry man she'd encountered in the barn. It seemed as if he was always hanging around the edges of her mind, waiting for a chance to slip in, tormenting her, taunting her with his superior smile.

Furiously she pressed the accelerator to the floor as though she could run from his mocking

73

features. The speedometer crept to fifty, passed fifty-five, and was edging sixty, when the wail of a siren brought her to her senses.

"Oh no!" she muttered. "Now I've done it! Just what I need, a speeding ticket."

Slowly she pulled the car over to the shoulder of the road and set the brake, nervously chewing her lower lip as she watched the policeman climb from the white car, its red light flashing. His broad ruddy face reflected a friendly authority as he came abreast of her car.

"In a bit of a hurry, Miss?" he asked with a trace of humor as he saw how shaken Cindy was. He motioned to the outside of the car. "Please step out and bring your license with you."

On shaking legs, Cindy slid from the car and handed him her driver's license. Her large green eyes met his squarely, although they held a trace of shame and a lot of embarrassment. "I'm sorry, Officer, I . . . . I guess my mind strayed and I didn't realize how fast I was going. It won't happen again, I promise."

"Young lady, I have a daughter who's just about your age and I'm going to talk to you the same way I would to her. Driving too fast on a dangerous road like this is foolish." His face had lost all traces of humor and showed only concern for what could have happened to her. "This car is too small and too light to hang to the curves. It could have flipped over with you before you knew it."

"I realize that now," Cindy answered contritely, the truth of his words registering in her expression.

The stocky policeman was swayed by her obvious sincerity. "All right, Miss Kelly," he said, handing back her license. "I'm going to let you off with a warning this time, but don't let it happen again. Always keep your attention on the road with an eye to your speed. Daydreaming and driving don't mix."

Cindy's attention was caught by an approaching truck over his left shoulder. Something about it looked vaguely familiar. For one thing, it could do with a good washing. As the truck closed the distance between them, her eyes widened. It couldn't be, but it *was*! Jed McCord.

Traveling a respectable fifty-five, the truck pulled around them. With an imprudent grin and salute, Jed sailed by.

Cindy was mortified as well as incensed. Every time she found herself in an embarrassing situation he happened along. She was seething as she watched the truck rapidly disappear into the distance. Her eyes narrowed as she saw his brake lights glow when he slowed for a curve. Only one was working and as she observed his, the scowl on her face faded as a mischievous glee brightened her spirits.

"Why, Officer—" she pointed ahead—"that truck has only one brake light. Is that legal?" Her thick black lashes fluttered and innocent concern shone in her emerald green eyes.

"It sure isn't," the policeman replied, thrusting the warning ticket at her, obviously anxious to get to his car. "You keep your speed down and watch what you're doing from now on. No more day-dreaming!"

"Oh, yes, I'll be careful," Cindy answered sweetly, and she dimpled with pleasure as the patrol car sped from the edge of the road, siren screaming and red light flashing.

Cindy pulled carefully back onto the highway.

After a glance at the rear-view mirror, she looked like the green-eyed cat that swallowed the canary, and she didn't mind at all as she resumed her trip toward Lexington.

The flashing red light up ahead brought a cheerful smile to her face. As she neared the patrol car and truck, pulled over just as she'd been a few minutes before, she couldn't resist the impulse to slow to a mere crawl as she flashed a mocking smile at Jed McCord. With an airy flutter of fingertips she sailed on by.

The pleasure of seeing the great Jed McCord stopped by the police stayed with her all the way into the city. She'd been extra careful with her speed, knowing how infuriating it would be if she were stopped again. This was one time she'd come out on top, and she liked the feeling.

With time to spare, she pulled into her allotted parking space at the Ames Agency, and with a graceful stride she entered the office. Once she was there she drew a deep breath and sat at her desk, trying to muster the courage to press the button on the office intercom. If Mr. Ames were free she'd turn in her resignation at once, to give him more time to find a new girl. She could soften the blow by offering to help train her before her two-weeks' notice was up.

Mentally she rehearsed the words she'd speak. She'd tell him she'd been wrong; it wasn't possible to commute from Pine Valley after all. The daily trips were strenuous and had began to affect her work. The pace she'd set for herself had proved to be too much and she had to come to a decision. It was either her life in the country or her job, and now that she'd had a taste of the quiet country life she didn't want to give it up.

She couldn't put it off any longer, but it was a reluctant hand that reached for the switch. Just as she was about to touch it, it buzzed loudly.

"Cindy, may I talk to you in my office?" Mr. Ames' voice was jovial as it bubbled from the small box.

"Right away," she replied, wondering at his apparently high spirits. Now was the time to talk to him too, but oh how she dreaded doing it. She tapped hesitantly at his office door, then slowly entered.

With a perplexed expression, she watched her stout little employer bustle from behind his desk and solicitously pull up a chair. After she was seated to his satisfaction, he returned to his chair and leaned back to beam from behind his gold-rimmed glasses. He entwined short pudgy fingers and a happy smile lighted his face.

"Cindy, I have some news that I think you may like. I know how much you enjoy living in Pine Valley, so how would you feel about working there?"

Cindy was astonished!

"The agency has been commissioned to draw up contracts on land sales in that area. Since you are already established down there, we'd like you to handle the office in Pine Valley."

She stared at Mr. Ames, utterly speechless. She'd entered the room prepared to quit her job to look for work in the valley, and here was Mr. Ames unknowingly solving her dilemma. Cindy had never believed in a guardian angel before, but the way things were turning out she was beginning to wonder.

Mistaking her silence for refusal, Mr. Ames was flustered. "Now, Cindy, don't turn me down," he wheedled. "I have every confidence in you. Besides, we don't have anyone else competent to send out there." In the face of her continued silence, he was becoming more edgy and nervous as he hovered over her and waited for her answer.

She was surprised at his agitation. The Pine Valley agency must be very important to him, she surmised. She smiled and quickly put an end to his worries. "I appreciate the confidence you have in me, Mr. Ames, and if you think I can handle the job, then I'll accept."

Upon hearing this, her timorous employer drew a long sigh of relief. "You don't know how pleased this makes me. The commission will bring a lot of money into the agency." His elation caused him to ramble. "When the offer was made, it was with the stipulation that you handle everything down there. I knew you'd accept . . . although Mr. McCord had his doubts."

"Wait!" Cindy interrupted, a sinking feeling in her stomach as comprehension dawned. "The contract is with the McCord Company? We'll handle the buying of right-of-way for the road, right? After that my job will end, because when the road is completed, they won't need us, will they?"

"Oh, yes, we'll have a permanent office there," Mr. Ames hurriedly assured her. "There'll be a lot of business for a real estate agency in that area. Please don't change your mind! The agency needs this contract, and McCord was emphatic; you're the only person he'll accept."

Suddenly his look changed from pleading to puzzlement. "Although I don't know why he was so insistent. Do you know Mr. McCord?"

Cindy was torn between a burning rage against

Jed and pity for Mr. Ames. She didn't see how she could turn down the job when the agency obviously depended on her. Guardian angel, indeed; more like a scheming devil. While her thoughts turned this way and that, Mr. Ames looked at her expectantly.

"Yes, I'm acquainted with Mr. McCord," she admitted dryly.

"Great!" he exclaimed, missing her tone entirely. "That means you'll be starting out on the right foot. It always pays to be friends with the people you work with."

Cindy was tempted to tell her boss he'd misunderstood. She'd said she knew Jed McCord, not that they were friends. They would never be friends, not if she had anything to do with it. But she couldn't bring herself to break the bright bubble of excitement that surrounded Mr. Ames. No, she wouldn't tell him of the antagonism that flared every time she and Jed McCord were together. It would worry him needlessly and to no purpose, since she had accepted the job.

Cindy spent the rest of the day alternating between one office and another, lining things up so she could make the transition from Lexington to Pine Valley as smoothly as possible.

Gradually her state of mind had calmed down to where she could contemplate working for the McCord Company. She would handle the job as efficiently as possible and do her best to stay out of that overbearing man's way. She brightened at the possibility that Ben Kindrick would be working with her. Maybe she was worrying for nothing. After all, Jed McCord didn't care for her any more than she did for him.

The hours passed swiftly and before she knew it

the time had come to meet Brent. The restaurant was more than five blocks away and she'd have to hurry. She gave the office a final glance to make sure all the work was put away and everything was tidy. Satisfied, she waved goodby to Mr. Ames through his open door and was on her way to meet her ex-fiance.

The posh restaurant Brent had chosen wasn't crowded yet but Cindy knew the place had to be a favorite of the cocktail crowd or he wouldn't have asked her to meet him there.

As she stood in the foyer looking out over the white-linen-covered tables, she caught sight of him immediately. His tall figure and almost pretty good looks drew attention no matter where he was.

At the moment he was engrossed in conversation with a svelte young brunette, and as she watched he picked up the dazzled girl's hand and brushed a feathery kiss across her palm. His smile was boyish, showing his flashing white teeth, and Cindy could see the girl melt under his charm.

Typically Brent, she thought with bitter, ironic amusement. He'll never change! For the moment he seemed to have forgotten her. Butterflies churned inside her as she wondered if she'd forgotten the feelings she'd had for him.

Delaying the inevitable meeting, she turned to the mirror that covered one wall of the foyer and was reassured by the image reflected in the large shining glass. Her white silk blouse and short black vest, combined with the smart gray skirt with the fashionable slit in the front, and her black leather boots, were very chic. With her self-confidence returned, she turned back to the room, drew a deep breath, and with a graceful stride crossed over to where Brent stood.

"Hello, Brent," she said coolly as she stepped up to the table.

"Cindy, sweetheart!" He turned from the other girl as though she didn't exist and Cindy felt a moment of sympathy, as hurt and disappointment flickered on her delicate features. Brent used his magnetic appeal as though it were a weapon and he was oblivious to the results.

"Brent!" The girl's plaintive tone as she clutched Brent's arm made Cindy wince. She felt a sudden urge to warn her against Brent, to tell her of the heartache in store if she persisted in her so apparent feelings for him. But she realized it would do no good, so she turned silently away.

"I'll talk to you tomorrow," Brent said, dismissing her with a lofty wave of his hand.

"But Brent . . . . " She couldn't seem to believe he was dismissing her.

"I said tomorrow!" His voice had deepened with impatience. With a gesture of cruel intent, he turned his back to her in order to concentrate on Cindy. The shattered girl hastened from the room, her eyes bright with unshed tears.

"Who is she, Brent?" Cindy asked quietly, her eyes following the slight figure.

"Just a girl from the office," he answered quickly. "Forget about her. I'm delighted to see you, although it's obvious that your stay in that godforsaken country has agreed with you. You're more beautiful than ever, which I didn't think possible." He flicked her shapely nose. "You've even gotten freckles from all that sun."

"Well, you know what they say about country sunshine," she said. "It's great, even in the fall."

"It sounds as though you've enjoyed living down there," he said. A lost look appeared in his brown eyes and he looked down at his hands. "I don't suppose you missed me at all."

Cindy was caught by the unhappiness in his voice and it tugged at her heart. "Of course I missed you, Brent," she said, laying her hand on his. "You were a part of my life and, no matter what has happened, I won't forget the happiness we had."

"We did have some good times, didn't we?" His tone was wistful, but then it turned bitter. "But I took care of that."

"It doesn't matter, Brent." Cindy hadn't thought that she would ever feel anything for him again, but now as she sat across from him a tiny doubt nagged her and she still wasn't sure of her feelings.

"Yes, it does matter," he said. A faint smile touched the corners of his mouth but didn't change the look in his eyes. "It matters to me. I took the only good part of my life and threw it away," he said. "And now I'll regret it forever."

"Brent." Cindy watched him closely. "I don't know how much of this is real and how much is your love of theatrics, but if you mean any of it, then you *have* changed. Maybe the experience has been good for both of us. At least we grew up."

"Yes, I can see you've matured," he agreed, assessing her with his eyes. "You're not a girl any more and I can be held to account for that."

"Oh, Brent." She smiled at him. "I consider that an asset, not a drawback. Everyone has to grow up sometime. But if you really want to know the truth, I still have a long way to go."

"Well, don't do it too quickly. I'd miss the girl

who still believes in dreams." His teasing grin held a trace of the Brent she used to know and she was glad to see it there.

The silence stretched between them and she was disconcerted to realize that they were still holding hands. She pulled her hand away and toyed with the candleholder on the table. She stared down at the table and her dark lashes covered the nervous expression in her green eyes.

"Cindy." Brent broke the uncomfortable lull. "Are you truly happy? I mean alone and all . . . ." His voice trailed lamely away.

"Are *you* happy, Brent?" She was aware that she really did want to know. It hadn't been an idle question.

"Oh, I go to parties and out with the crowd, but I don't enjoy myself like we used to. But you know me," he said, shifting around in his chair. "I'll always be out there trying."

Cindy was glad to discover he wasn't enjoying the night life as much as he had before. Maybe someday he'd get over his desire to always be where the bright lights were. And maybe someday he'd give country life a try.

"Do you . . . do you date now?" she asked, the words tumbling from her lips, and even she was surprised by the question. Stumbling over her words, she tried to turn it into casual conversation. "I mean . . . well . . . the girl . . . . I thought that the girl you were talking to when I came in might be someone special."

"No, although I'm ashamed of the way I treated her," he admitted ruefully. "I've dated her before and she does seem to have some feelings for me. But when I looked up and saw you, I was afraid you'd get the wrong impression. See, that's called a guilty conscience. I'm still trying to hide my flirtations from you."

His awareness of these self-truths surprised her. The old Brent would never have admitted that he flirted, much less confess that he tried to hide it. She found she liked this new Brent and wondered if this night might bring a new beginning.

The waiter hovered next to the table, waiting impatiently for them to order. Noticing this, Brent turned to him and said, "We'll only have drinks for now. I'll have Scotch and the lady will have white wine."

"I haven't been away too long. You still remember what I drink."

"I've never forgotten what a lady drinks. That's one of my most infallible charms," he said with a crooked grin.

"That's true." She nodded. "I'd almost forgotten."

The waiter arrived at their table and served the drinks with a flourish. To add to the romantic atmosphere, he lit the candle and then vanished.

"All we need now is the violins," Brent said wryly, as he picked up his drink.

Warm memories came flooding back to her and she remember how it had been before. There had been violins and moonlight, roses and romantic dinners, declarations of endless love and the deep heady feelings of being wanted and cherished. That's what was missing from her life, she thought, and that was why she hadn't been completely happy in the country. She'd missed the joy that came with sharing her life with someone she loved.

"Cindy, is there any chance we might get back

together? I've missed all the good times we've shared," he said, almost as if he'd read her thoughts.

Her heart lurched painfully. She had come to return his ring, to end things between them forever. But now, old feelings were beginning to stir and she was confused. She watched him through lowered lashes. Had he really changed? she asked herself. And would she ever be able to forget the heartache he'd caused?

"I don't know," she said, shaking her head. "I want to put the past behind me but I truly don't know if you can be part of my future."

"I know I drove you away." His voice reflected regret. "And I'll never be able to make it up to you, but if reasons can make a difference, then I want to explain."

"Don't, Brent," she begged. "I'd rather not talk about it."

"Cindy, you can't hide from the truth," he said, holding tightly to her hand. She could see from his eyes that he had to talk about it. He had to explain. It was the only way to salvage his conscience.

"I suppose you're right," she relented. "But I can't promise this will change things."

Brent's eyes were relieved but reluctant as he swirled the ice in his drink. He raised the glass to his lips and swallowed deeply, as if to delay the words he had to say.

"First of all, you mustn't think I took her to our apartment," he said. "Even if it had been planned, which it wasn't," he added quickly. "I'd never have taken her there."

"Why was she there?" Cindy asked painfully.

"It happened just as I said," he continued. "She came over to show me where the fuse box was and

I offered her a drink. I swear, I was only being friendly to a neighbor."

"She spoke as though that hadn't been the first time," she reminded him quietly. "And she said she was glad I'd found out."

"Well . . . I had stopped in at her apartment a few times," he admitted, avoiding her eyes. "Remember the day I had off and I painted the kitchen in the apartment?" At her nod, he rushed on, "That was the first time I met her. She works at the Paradise Cocktail Lounge at night and she's home during the day. Anyway, she invited me over for coffee and I went. I know I shouldn't have gone, but it wasn't a big deal, just a cup of coffee."

"She never invited me over for coffee. As a matter of fact, she barely spoke when we met in the hall," Cindy observed wryly.

Brent let her remark pass without comment as he drained the last of his Scotch. Then with a quick snap of his fingers at the waiter, he ordered a refill.

"She's a divorcee," he went on, as though there had been no pause at all, "And she lives alone . . . . Then it got to be a habit—whenever I visited our apartment alone I'd drop in for coffee with her. She was lonely and I was company for her. Things went on that way until that day in our apartment. The fuse had gone out and I went over to ask her where the box was."

"Oh, Brent," Cindy said.

"I know . . . it would have happened sooner or later," he said, dropping his eyes. "Things were just naturally headed that way. And I can't even say I didn't realize it, because I did. To tell the truth, I wanted it that way."

Cindy's green eyes were wide with anguish.

"You wanted it to happen."

His second drink arrived at their table and he picked it up. "You have to understand: I'm a man, with a man's desires and needs. You were my fiance and I'd placed you on a pedestal. You were young and she was a woman of experience. I'd never intended to hurt you. I didn't think you'd find out."

"Oh God," she exclaimed softly, "I was so naive."

"No," he disagreed, with a slight twist of his lips, "just innocent."

There was a poignant silence as Brent finished his Scotch. The glass of white wine sat untouched before her, as his words whirled around in her mind. He had spoken the truth and, although she didn't like him very much for it, she had to respect him because he hadn't tried to hide himself from blame.

"You haven't touched your wine," Brent said, gesturing toward her glass. "But I think I'll have another Scotch."

It was then that Cindy noticed his speech was getting thick and his old confidence was beginning to return. His quick consumption of the Scotch was having an effect.

"Don't you think you've had enough?" she asked, keeping her voice low. Her eyes were troubled as she watched him shake his head and grin.

"Same old Cindy," he drawled, amused. "You're still trying to take care of me, aren't you?"

"It looks as if someone should," she answered lightly, as he beckoned over her head to the waiter. She saw the man flash Brent a look of disapproval, but his manner remained courteous and he nodded to his request.

"By the way," he said, "I heard the new highway that's going through Pine Valley has confiscated your little farm." There was a slight edge to his words and Cindy thought she detected a hint of satisfaction on his face.

"You don't have to be so satisfied," she responded, and her doubts on returning his ring were beginning to fade. "I put a lot into that place and it hurt when I lost it."

"I know that, honey," Brent said, and he tried to look sympathetic. "But it's really for the best. You have your investment back, maybe a little more, and you can come home where you belong. The country isn't for you. It never was."

Shock held Cindy in its rigid grip as she realized he thought she was home to stay. It had never entered his mind that she would do anything else. He was the second man in just a matter of days who'd managed to cast doubts on her sincerity and capabilities of making her way in the country. Well, she'd show them! She was made of sterner stuff than either of them gave her credit for.

"What do you think I should do, Brent, come home and pick up when we left off? Should I forget all about my life down there?" She was exasperated, and showed it.

Brent was well into his third glass of Scotch and his actions were becoming uncoordinated. He gestured with force. "Well, damn it, why not? You still have my ring and you know I want you. Sure we have problems, but most people do. We'll work them out, but we can't do that if you plan on staying in that place."

"*That* place is called Pine Valley and I like it." She was beginning to get angry.

Brent decided to try a different approach. "What did you do for entertainment?" he asked. "There are no restaurants, night clubs, nothing. You had to be bored to tears."

"Night clubs and restaurants and going out aren't the most important things in life, Brent." She was beginning to see him in a new light. All he wanted from life was a good time.

"Of course they're not," he said, humoring her. "But it's stimulating and interesting to be with people of intelligence, people with class. Don't tell me you don't miss being with your own kind."

It's funny, she mused as she listened to his words. He's so vain, it never occurred to him that we might really be finished. All that he said was meant only to smooth the reconciliation. He believes everything will work out his way. He's so shallow and selfish he'll never care for anyone more than for himself.

Leaning back in her chair, she took a long look at the man she'd almost married. The brightness of his personality, and his charm, had attracted her in the first place, and he was undeniably handsome, but she also realized he was shallow, conceited and almost blatantly self-oriented.

"A penny for your thoughts, darling." Brent's words were slightly slurred, the aftermath of his drinks. "You're certainly quiet. Has living in the boondocks cost you the knack of polite conversation?" The faintly patronizing tone that had crept into his voice irritated her. "Marge and Bob are having a party tonight and we don't want to be late, so would you mind looking at the menu?"

"You're taking too much for granted, Brent," she said, amazed at the depths of his self-confidence. He had been so sure they would be together again that he'd planned for them to go to a party that night. "I'm having dinner with my parents tonight, and I won't be able to go to Marge and Bob's party."

"Call your parents; they'll understand. Now that you're home they can see you any time."

"No, Brent, you don't understand. I'm going back to Pine Valley and I'm going to stay. I came only to return this." Reaching into her purse, she put the velvet box on the table.

"Have you taken leave of your senses? Do you really think you'll be happy in that little jerkwater town with a bunch of hillbillies?" His comely face twisted scornfully. "I warn you, I won't wait forever while you waste your time playing house down there."

"Brent, I don't want you to wait. We'd never be happy together; we're too different. We don't have anything in common any more and I'm not sure we ever did."

"You still can't forgive me for one indiscretion, can you?" Brent asked with a theatrical sigh. "It'll never happen again, I swear to you."

"I know you believe that now, Brent, but I don't think it's possible for you to be faithful. I'm just glad it happened before we were married." With a slender finger she pushed the ring box toward him. "It's a beautiful ring, but it wasn't meant for me."

"What's happened, baby?" His vanity was wounded. Then he sneered, "Have you fallen for one of the local clods down there? Maybe I'm not the only one who's been playing around."

"I don't have to sit here and listen to this. I'm leaving!" Anger colored her cheeks as she pushed away from the table.

"Go! Go back to the sticks, go back to your little shack in the hills. Is that where the local bucks line up? Maybe that's where all the action is . . ." Brent's vicious tirade continued, his voice getting louder and louder.

Heads were turning in their direction. A waitress stood by with an open mouth and at the next table two elderly ladies tittered nervously.

Cindy's green eyes sparkled dangerously. "Don't judge me by your standards, Brent. Not everyone is as lacking in morals as you are!"

Blindly she left the table, holding her head high as she threaded her way past openly staring people.

SEVEN

Almost lightheaded with relief, Cindy pressed the buzzer of her parents' apartment door. The confrontation with Brent had unsettled her, but she was confident she had done the right thing. Now he was in her past and she didn't intend to let his opinions of her life in Pine Valley affect her. She would prove to herself that she was serious about living in Pine Valley and neither Brent nor Jed McCord could stop her.

The door opened and her father clasped her in his arms with a happy smile. "Mother, Cindy's here!" he called in the direction of the kitchen. Her mother bustled into the living room, drying her hands on the end of her apron.

"Hello, honey," she said, hugging the daughter who looked so much like her but whose personality was definitely her husband's. "Dinner will be ready in just a few minutes. How is everything going in Pine Valley? You don't come to see us often enough and those little notes you call letters never tell us anything important."

"Oh, Mom, you know how I am about writing letters. I save everything interesting so I can tell you about it when I come into town." Cindy felt wonderful just being with the two people she loved most in the world.

"How about you women seeing if you can't get dinner on the table while you catch up on the news." Her father smiled, winking at Cindy as he returned to his favorite chair and picked up the evening paper.

"Come on, Mom," Cindy said, smiling fondly at her father. "You know Dad's not sociable until he's caught up with the news."

The kitchen smelled heavenly and, as her mother peered into the oven, Cindy peered over her shoulder. "Umm . . . pot roast, my favorite." Her face lighted with a pixie smile. "I haven't smelled anything so deliciously tempting since the last time I was here."

"There's cherry cheesecake for dessert." Her mother smiled, her eyes twinkling. "Now you can make the salad."

Cindy stood at the sink washing the salad greens and listening to her mother's news of family and friends. The conversation was pleasant. Then her mother asked, "Now tell me, have you found a new place with your friend Jan?"

"Oh yes, and it's really nice and I know you'll be glad to hear it has a bathroom, electricity and all the unnecessary stuff," Cindy answered.

"I'm glad!" Mrs. Kelly exclaimed. "I could never understand how you thought you could live without them. You weren't brought up to do without the essentials of life."

"Oh Mom, don't you start on me too. I've had enough people tell me I'm too soft to live in the country. I love it and it didn't bother me at all to rough it down there. At least not very much."

"Who are all these people who say you're not strong enough to make it down there?" her mother inquired, indignantly. She could say it, but no one else should. Secretly she was proud of her daughter's determination to live the way she wanted, and if it made Cindy happy, that was all that counted.

"Brent for one. I returned his ring this afternoon and he wasn't very happy with my decision."

"Brent." Her mother sniffed disdainfully. "I've never meddled into your affairs, Cindy, but I'm going to say this now. That man is nothing but trouble and I'm glad the romance is finished. He hurt you, but that was nothing compared to the heartache in store for you if you had married him."

"I know, Mom. I'm sorry if I caused you worry." Cindy darted an apologetic smile over her shoulder.

"I didn't worry too much," her mother disclaimed, running her hand along the faded copper hair above her temple. "I had a feeling you would wake up before it was too late. You've got too much sense to settle for a good-time fellow like Brent."

"Why, Mother," Cindy teased, "I never knew you had so much confidence in my good sense."

"I've always had confidence in you, Cindy." Her mother smiled with pride. "Now if only you'd learn to control your temper, you'd be perfect."

"I'm doing better, Mom. Why I've only quarreled with Jed McCord once since I last saw you. But, oh, you should have seen him this morning!" She grinned with delight as she recounted her encounter with the policeman and her part in getting Jed pulled over because of his broken tail light.

"Cindy!" Her mother was shocked. "I don't want to hear of you driving that fast again. And that was a terrible thing to do to Mr. McCord."

"Aw, Mom, don't worry about him. He can take care of himself. Jed McCord thinks he's so smart. I hope he got a ticket; it wouldn't hurt him. He has plenty of money, I hear. But it would have wounded his pride."

"I don't care if he does have money. That's not the point," Mrs. Kelly scolded. "I wouldn't have thought you'd be so petty."

"I wasn't being petty," Cindy cried, stung by the disappointed look her mother gave her. "He drove past and gloated when he saw me stopped by the police. All I did was return the favor."

"That's a prime example of your temper getting out of control." Her mother's eyes were reproachful. "How did you know he was gloating?"

"You don't know the man, Mother!" Savagely she tore the greens and crammed them into the large salad bowl. "He enjoys seeing me humiliated."

"You know, Cindy," Mrs. Kelly said thoughtfully, "I'm beginning to think you enjoy fighting with this man."

Cindy burst out laughing. "If that's enjoyment, then I guess I'm going to have a ball from now on. Mr. Ames is setting up an office in Pine Valley in conjunction with the McCord Company and I'll be in charge of it. That means I'll be working with Jed McCord every day."

"That means you won't be coming to town every day then, I suppose." Her mother tried not to show her feelings as she lifted the roasting pan from the oven.

"Oh Mom, don't look so woebegone. I'll come up on weekends."

"It's hard for me to realize my little girl is grown up and living away from home, that's all."

Cindy gave her mother a hug. "I love you and Dad and I miss you a lot, so I'll be around, probably more than you want."

"Don't be a goose; your father and I want you home every chance you get. Now set the table before he starts complaining about dinner being late."

The meal was delicious and Cindy ate all her favorite dishes with pleasure as she regaled her parents with glowing descriptions of her new home. Her father was keenly interested as she described the farm.

"It sounds as if it could be my grandparents' farm," he said, "although it's a long way from where they lived. Just hearing about the barn and the fields brings back memories of when I was a child and spent my summers there. It's been a long time."

"Dad, you and Mother will have to come down and visit us. Jan would love it and so would I!" Cindy's eyes shone as she appealed to him. "I'd get a kick out of showing you the town and the farm and everything."

"We'll come, won't we, Ginnie?" He turned to her mother and smiled.

"How could I resist two of you at once?" Her mother's expression was pleased. "Yes, we'll go, maybe this weekend. But just for one day. Maybe next spring we'll spend more time and Dad can do some fishing."

By the time Cindy fell asleep in her old room that night, the plans for her parents' visit to Pine Valley were all set and she was looking forward to having them meet her new friends and neighbors.

The week flew by and Saturday dawned in the valley bright and clear. She and Jan had made plans to meet her parents in town and show them around before taking them out to Jaggie Jenson's farm. From there she'd take them up to the cabin. It would probably be the last chance they'd have to see it before it was torn down.

Mr. and Mrs. Kelly fell in love with the town and Jan impressed them with her bubbling good humor. They enjoyed their trip to the country. The only awkward moment during their visit came when Cindy and Jan treated them to lunch at the diner. As they started in the door, they met Jed and Ben, who were returning to work after the lunch hour.

"Miss Kelly," Ben said, doffing his cap and smiling at her mother.

"Mr. Kindrick, Mr. McCord," Cindy said stiffly as she tried to usher her mother through the door.

"Mr. McCord?" her mother exclaimed, turning back to Jed and Ben. "We've heard so much about you from Cindy. I'm glad we've finally had a chance to meet you." She turned and pulled Cindy's father forward. "This is Mr. McCord, James. You know, the one who bought the cabin."

Jed shot a quick look of amusement at Cindy's pink cheeks as he and Ben shook hands with her father. "I hope your daughter has spoken well of me, but I doubt it. We don't see eye to eye on anything."

Her mother's face told her she instintively liked Jed as she sparkled up at him and confided, "Cindy's temper flares, but she never stays mad long."

"Mother!" Cindy cried, her face bright red.

Jed spoke smoothly. "I'd better get back to work before your daughter loses her temper with me again. It was nice meeting you both and I hope you enjoy your visit in Pine Valley."

Cindy finally got her mother seated in the diner and, as her father smiled sympathetically at her across the table, she shook her head in mock despair. She loved her mother dearly, but she had to admit there were times when she felt like disowning her.

"Why Cindy," Mrs. Kelly said as she scanned the menu, "you didn't tell me your Mr. McCord was so goodlooking."

"He's not *my* Mr. McCord, Mother!" Cindy said, exasperated. "Please forget about him and let's decide what to order."

"Yes, Ginnie, leave the girl alone and don't tease her about *her* Mr. McCord any more." Her father's eyes twinkled and he winked at Jan.

"You're all impossible," she said, trying hard to look stern, but her green eyes sparkled with humor and suddenly they all burst out laughing.

EIGHT

The bright colorful days of September passed and October made its chilly debut with a hint of winter to come. The rose arbor at the corner of Maggie Jenson's house held only the withered remnants of summer's once glorious blooms and the tall willow tree stood stark and bare.

But Cindy and Jan didn't notice the advancing signs of winter. They were too busy spending all their free time in the house. Together they worked, laughed and talked, and their friendship had blossomed into a closeness that even few sisters share. Together they papered the walls, and laughter rang through the empty rooms as Cindy discovered the fun of working with someone else.

She'd begun to realize that although she really did love the country, the life of a hermit wasn't for her. The little cabin had filled a void in her heart and helped her through the bad times she'd had after she and Brent had parted, and she'd always love the memory of it. But equally she loved the new house and the companionship of Jan.

The girls hastened to finish all their projects before Cindy's time ran out at the cabin. She took pleasure in telling Jan that Jed was cruel and heartless, without a shred of respect for anything but power and money. She doubted if he would wait one minute after the deadline to start knocking the place down. Jan didn't agree, but after seeing Cindy's anger at the mention of Jed's name, she didn't protest.

Soon the Saturday rolled around when they planned to move Cindy's belongings down to their new house. She stood on the cabin porch that morning and watched Jan's yellow bug come bouncing up the drive, followed by a clean blue pickup truck. And behind the truck she was surprised to note Arthur's big car.

"I brought help!" Jan called merrily, as she waved the truck around her Volkswagen. "Hank and Arthur are going to help us and we'll picnic down by the swimming hole."

"Okay," Cindy agreed, "but it's not a very good day for picnicking."

"It'll warm up," the ever-optimistic Jan replied. "And if it doesn't we'll build a fire!"

"Here, then earn your keep!" Hank threw a big empty box off the truck in Jan's direction. She caught it with ease.

Cindy watched as Jan and Hank smiled at each other in the special way of people in love. They were ideal for each other and she hoped Hank would soon be able to overcome the mental block he had about getting married. Jan loved him and aspired only to make a home for him and to have lots of babies. Of course it would mean she'd lose Jan as a housemate, but she would still like to see Jan's life complete.

"Don't worry about them. They'll make it!" Arthur's voice at her elbow made her turn and grin.

"How did you know what I was thinking?" she asked, surprised at his insight.

"You always have a certain look on your face when you're concerned about someone you care for," he stated quietly, his brown eyes serious behind the heavy-framed glasses. "You're even more beautiful when you turn introspective."

"Thank you, kind sir!" Cindy made an exaggerated curtsey. "Shall we rejoin yon peasants?"

Arthur laughed at her frivolity. "I'm glad you're not letting this get you down," he said, waving his arm in the direction of the house. "I was afraid you'd be very upset."

Cindy was touched by his thoughtfulness. Gently she touched his hand. "Is that why you're here, to give me moral support?"

"That and more," Arthur answered truthfully. "I'd like you to go to a movie with me tonight."

"Jan and Hank are going too. Why don't we all go together?"

"Let's see what they're up to and we'll ask them." Arthur grinned down at her, his eyes admiring the way her hair shone in the sun.

Cindy picked up one of the boxes and sauntered to the cabin, a bemused Arthur in tow.

"Cindy, we're packing the dishes," Jan said from the kitchen door. "Boy, will we need these! I never did any cooking at the boardinghouse and I don't have any kitchen utensils at all."

"Did you hear that, Hank?" Cindy teased. "She can't cook, so after you two get married you'll have to send her to cooking school."

"Oh Cindy," Jan protested, giggling, "I *can* cook and you know it! I make the best canned biscuits in the county."

101

"I'm not marrying her for her cooking," Hank said solemnly. "I'm marrying her to take care of my little ones."

"Oh, Hank," Jan breathed, delighted, "that's the first time you've mentioned children!" Her plump little face was glowing.

"I'm not talking about kids," Hank drawled, as he winked at Cindy and Arthur. "I'm talking about Barney and Sam, the best darn coon dogs in the state."

"Hank Farley!" Jan cried goodnaturedly, whacking him with the towel she held in her hand. "I'll feed Barney and Sam their last meal, too!"

Leaving Jan and Hank after that last bit of horseplay, Cindy and Arthur began clearing the shelves in the living room.

"Now answer my question," Arthur said as she packed books into the large box.

Cindy leaned back on her heels and peered up at him questioning. "What question?"

"How you really feel about leaving this cabin. You're not going to let it get you down, are you?" His worried eyes watched her intently.

"I was broken up when I lost this place," Cindy admitted quietly. "But after finding friends like you, Jan and Hank, I've come to see that a house isn't everything. But I still wish I could move the house somewhere to keep it safe. I hate the thought of its being torn down. It had its own little magic for me and it's a shame to have it smashed, then buried in the ground."

"I feel that way too!" Arthur smiled at her. "The magic part, I mean. After all, it brought you to the valley, didn't it?"

Cindy looked away from the naked yearning in his eyes. "Arthur, I'm very glad we're friends, but please don't get serious. After Brent, I'm not ready for another relationship except friendship." She looked up at him beseechingly, her green eyes wide.

Beguiled by her beauty, Arthur could deny her nothing. Throwing up his hands he said, "Friends it is, but if you ever change your mind, let me know, okay?"

A sweep of dark lashes hid the relief Cindy felt at Arthur's promise. "Thank you," she murmured softly.

"Cindy?" Jan's voice relieved them from the sticky moment. "Let's go down to the old swimming hole, okay? It's hotter than blazes, and we can finish packing later."

"Let's do," Cindy answered eagerly. "You men go build a fire and Jan and I will dig out some hotdogs and we'll have a cookout—that is, if Jan didn't pack the food," she added, laughing.

"No way!" Jan tittered. "You know me better than that! Although. . . ." Ruefully she glanced down at her plump figure. "I should watch what goes in my mouth. I wish I were as slender as you, Cindy."

"Hush, woman, I love you just the way you are!" Hank said as he slid a lanky arm around her shoulder. He looked down at her and his Adam's apple bobbed convulsively. "Cindy's figure is fine, but so is yours. Now quit fretting and get the food. I'm starved!"

Jan basked in the warm admiration Hank displayed, and as the tall gangling farmer grinned down at the buxom girl, Cindy knew Arthur was right: they would make it just fine.

The young women chattered aimlessly as they filled a basket to take down to the men. Hotdogs, chips, buns, a bowl of potato salad, some fresh fruit and a large jug of iced tea went into the basket. A tablecloth on top and they were ready to go.

"This should fill them up." Jan grinned. "Then after we feed them we'll really put them to work."

"Jan," Cindy replied, shaking her bright head and laughing, "you're a slavedriver, you know."

"I know one thing," Jan said, tilting her smiling face in the general direction of the creek. "If we don't get down there, those two are liable to set the woods on fire."

"Let's hurry," Cindy said cheerfully. "But you're not worried about their burning the woods to the ground. It's clear that you can't stay away from Hank, that's all. So take the basket and run."

"Oh, Cindy, does it show that much?" Jan was serious now. "I wouldn't want Hank to think I'm desperate."

"Jan, don't be a silly goose! Hank loves the attention you give him. And I have a feeling there's going to be a wedding in the valley real soon."

"Do you think so?" Jan asked doubtfully.

"Yes, I think so," Cindy said firmly. "Now get down there and get them busy. I'll dig out some plates and eating utensils and bring them along."

Jan impulsively hugged her friend, then wordlessly dashed toward the creek.

Cindy watched from the kitchen window as Jan flitted across the yard and down the path. She was glad to see Jan in such high spirits and she found herself praying that nothing would happen to spoil the other girl's happiness.

She sighed as she turned from the window, then jumped involuntarily at a movement. Jed McCord was lounging against the kitchen door. His keen eyes appraised her with interest as he lazed against the doorjamb, his arms folded across his broad chest.

"You have a nasty habit of sneaking up on people," she said, ice dripping from her voice.

Indolently he grinned, amused at her words. "Sometimes a fellow sees some interesting sights if others don't know he's around."

Cindy blushed a deep fiery red. Confused, she turned back to the window, aware of trembling hands as well as flaming face. "You have your nerve!"

"I knocked on the door but you didn't hear me," he said affably, shifting his weight onto the other leg and managing to look very much at ease. "Your mind was on other things, I suppose. Anyway, the door was open so I came in."

"Do you barge into anyone's house, just because the door is open?" she asked with biting sarcasm.

"My house," he said softly, but the steely glint in his eyes belied his quiet tone. "You forget this is my house now."

"I don't know how I could," she cried, her green eyes flashing fire. "You always show up uninvited to remind me. Is that why you're here today?"

Jed's eyes narrowed to gray slits. "Forget the house!" he ordered as his stance in the doorway straightened with the force of his anger. "The Ames Agency has informed me that you'll be handling the contracts for them here in Pine Valley. That means we'll be sharing the field office for awhile."

"Yes, Mr. Ames told me how you maneuvered things to get me a job here in Pine Valley," Cindy answered, and watched his reaction to her words. "Was it your way of salvaging your conscience after you forced me from my home?"

Jed's eyes blazed and he stepped forward threat-eningly. For a moment Cindy was afraid she'd pushed him too far.

"Cindy?" Arthur's quiet voice cut into their heated exchange. His serious eyes traveled over Cindy with concern. Seeing her agitated state, he turned to Jed. "Is there a problem, McCord?" he asked coldly, as he placed a protective arm around Cindy's shoulders.

Jed's hard gray eyes flickered from Arthur's arm to Cindy's distressed face. "No problem at all," he answered, his voice clipped and his eyes locked with hers. "The office will be ready for you Monday and I'll expect you on the job at eight o'clock. If you think this is just a token job, Miss Kelly, I'm afraid you're in for a surprise!" Jed's hard tones rang through the small cabin.

Cindy nodded, unable to say a word in retort. Her eyes burned with unshed tears and she couldn't understand why it bothered her for Jed to see Arthur's arm around her, since she didn't care in the least what he thought about her.

As Cindy and Arthur walked down to the old swimming hole, she found herself prattling cheer-fully, too brightly, in her determination to enjoy the rest of the afternoon. This was one time Jed McCord wouldn't get her down.

Jan and Hank greeted them with absent smiles and she knew they wouldn't notice anything amiss. They were so wrapped up in each other they probably never realized that she and Arthur were around. But as she turned to smile at Arthur, she caught a look of speculation on his face that caused her to wonder what thoughts were running through his mind.

At last the day was over. Walking up from the creek, they discussed their plans for the movie. But Cindy begged off, explaining that she had a headache. Arthur assured her he understood, but as she darted a quick look at his expressionless face she had a feeling he was talking about more than just the headache. The knowing look he gave her as the three of them started back to town bothered her for a long time.

Jan and Hank had promised to return the next day to move the last of her belongings to the new house, so she decided to put things in order around the little cabin for the last time. Although it really didn't matter, she realized with a pang. The house would be demolished as soon as she had everything out of it.

"Damn Jed McCord!" Her voice blazed in the silence. The frustrations of the day had caught up with her and she hurled the picnic basket across the room. "Damn him, damn him . . . " she sobbed brokenly. Her pent-up emotions were released in a flood as she sat in the empty room and cried.

Finally the sobs dwindled away and she laughed weakly to discover she had the hiccups. Now that the storm had subsided, she began to gather up the leftovers strewn around the room, hiccuping all the while.

When she was standing over the trash can, the lid in midair, Jed's words came flooding back to her. He had made it clear that he expected her to work in his office. Monday . . . she'd be working with him . . . which meant there would be no end to the misery he'd inflict on her, just to get even for the way she'd talked to him. *He'd do it too, with great satisfaction.*

The only consolation she found in these

thoughts were that they'd frightened the hiccups right out of her.

NINE

Monday dawned dull and gloomy. A cold rain drizzled down the roof of Cindy's new home and dripped from the eaves of the porch. The last stubborn leaves that clung to the bare branches of the willow tree were beaten off by the wind and rain.

Cindy stood at the window and watched the water stream down the glass panes. "The first day in our new home and it has to rain!" she remarked plaintively, running long slender fingers along the small wood casings that divided the large window into diamond designs.

"Winter's not far off," Jan commented as she rinsed out her coffee cup at the sink. "That rain's cold, and it won't be long until Halloween. After that, cold weather will really set in."

"Well, let's get to work or we're both going to be late," Cindy said, as she gave the neat bun at the back of her head a pat. "I don't know about you," she said, frowning, "but my boss is going to make things miserable enough without my being late."

"You really *are* dreading this job, aren't you?" Jan asked.

"I sure am! You know how Jed McCord feels about me, and I'm not wild about him, either. To tell the truth, Jan, I don't think this is going to work out at all."

"Give it a chance," Jan advised. "It may not be as bad as you think."

"He's a chauvinist and I'm a shrew," Cindy said, grinning. "Do you really think it'll work?"

"I'm glad you've kept your sense of humor, because something tells me you're going to need it." Jan's eyes twinkled. "But who knows, you two may even turn out to be friends."

"Fat chance!" Cindy sniffed. "Do you think I'm dressed all right?" She straightened the jacket of the tailored tan pant suit, wondering if the blouse were too severe, the scarf a shade too much.

"You look beautiful. I've never seen that suit before. Is it new?" Jan asked, admiration in her eyes.

"Yes, and the scarf is too. I bought them the last time I was in Lexington. I spent too much, but I liked the outfit and I wanted to make a good impression on my first day," Cindy admitted.

"Ah ha! Trying to impress the boss?"

"That'll be the day," Cindy protested vehemently, her face pink. "But if looking my best will help him go easy on me, then I won't mind."

"Well, if we don't get out of here, neither of us is going to have a boss to impress," Jan said, grabbing up her jacket and purse. "We're already late!"

As Jan parked the little yellow Volkswagen in front of the hardware store, she turned to Cindy and reminded her, "Don't forget we promised to visit Millie Corry tonight. Sudie will be there too. They can hardly wait to meet you."

"Oh, shoot!" she grimaced. "I forgot! I'll be leaving work early today. I have a dentist's appointment at three."

"I could call Arthur and ride over with him after work," Cindy offered, "but only if you promise to be there. From the way you describe those two, I'll need you to run interference for me." Cindy spoke lightly, but she was just a bit serious. If those two old ladies were half as meddlesome as Jan seemed to believe she knew she'd need help.

"They're not that bad, but I'll be there before you," Jan promised, as she dashed from the car and ran through the rain to the hardware store.

Pulling her collar up against the pelting rain, Cindy splashed across the street to the McCord field office. It held a desk—which was the sum total of the Ames Agency in Pine Valley, at least for awhile. But Mr. Ames had assured her she'd have her own place of business as soon as a building could be located. Until then she'd have to make do.

Cindy glanced down at her watch as she opened the door and went in. Five minutes late. That wasn't too bad. She'd really thought it was later than that. She stopped just inside the door, shook the rain from her new jacket, and looked around the office where she'd be working.

One glance made it clear that only men had occupied the place. It was cluttered and messy, and dust covered every surface. It looked as if it had never been cleaned. Of the three desks in the large single office, only one was bare. The others were piled high with place books of the area, maps and papers. How they could find anything was beyond her.

Her eyes traveled around the room and settled with dismay on the hard features of her employer. He and Ben Kendrick were standing in front of a map of the valley that hung on the wall on the far side of the room.

Jed spoke with biting conciseness, "You're late. When I say eight I meant eight, not ten after! When you work for the McCord Company, you get to work on time."

"Aw now, Jed," Ben said uneasily, "aren't you being a little hard on her? After all, it's her first day on the job." The look Ben shot Cindy seemed to be a silent apology for Jed's brusque behavior.

Cynically Jed looked at Cindy, his carved features hard. "Don't tell me you've fallen under her spell too, Ben. It seems Miss Kelly has a way about her that makes men want to protect her. But don't concern yourself. With her disposition, she's well able to take care of herself!"

"Your disposition needs a little improvement too, Mr. McCord," Cindy snapped. "And you're right, I'm well able to protect myself, especially from the likes of you." Then her tone softened as she turned to Ben and said, "Thank you anyway, Mr. Kendrick."

"That's a nice outfit you have on, *Miss Kelly.*" Jed's face was impassive as he stood there watching her.

Cindy was surprised at his comment and her green eyes showed her emotions as they searched his face and wondered how she should react to what might, or might not, have been a compliment. The way he emphasized her name sounded ominous, but she settled on a demure, "Thank you."

Jed glanced at Ben and smiled crookedly. "Come on," he said, motioning Cindy to the door. "We've got to see some people about contracts. Take that portable typewriter and we'll get along."

Ben stepped forward in protest. "Jed, can't you put that off until tomorrow? The weather's bad and some of those places are a long way off the road."

"If she works for us, she does her job," Jed told him coldly, and his harsh attitude squelched any further comment from Ben. Throwing up his hands, Ben gave Jed a look of disapproval and slammed out the door.

Cindy turned and watched Ben leave the room, apprehensive. Lord, this job is going to be worse than I thought. McCord is an arrogant bully. If it weren't for Mr. Ames I'd quit right now. Without a word, she turned to the desk, picked up the typewriter, looked McCord straight in the eye and said, "I'm ready whenever you are, *Mr. McCord*." She made sure she put as much stress on his name as he had on hers. Feeling a twinge of satisfaction, she followed him to the door.

Cindy hesitated on the threshold, watching Jed as he crossed the sidewalk with long sure strides, ignoring the stinging rain. He reached the truck and, in one fluid motion, opened the door and settled behind the wheel. Through the blurred windshield he seemed to be watching her with cold detachment. So much for his concern, she told herself indignantly.

The rain fell harder, the fat drops splattering against the sidewalk. Water ran off the edge of the curb and rushed alongside the truck toward the gutter below. Wet, soggy leaves caught in the tumbling rush of water swirled round and round over the sewer before plunging down to be caught by the iron grate. Even as she watched, the foaming muddy water began to back up, flooding the street between her and the truck.

113

Cindy shot a bleak look at the impassive features of the man waiting in the truck. He had made it clear that he wasn't going to offer any assistance and the dirty water was getting deeper every second she hesitated. So, gritting her teeth and holding the hem of the trimly tailored slacks high, she waded through the muddy water to the pickup truck, jerked the door open and clambered inside, dragging the typewriter with her. Gingerly she slid her feet out of her sodden shoes and dumped the water that had accumulated in them out the door. As she glanced up she saw a flicker of impatience cross Jed's lean tanned face. His mouth tightened as a strong arm reached across her and pulled the door shut.

"Thanks for nothing," she muttered disdainfully, wrinkling her pert nose.

"You said you could take care of yourself," he said, a mocking inflection in his tone, as he started the engine. With total indifference to her dripping state, he shifted into first gear and headed out of town.

Cindy set her teeth stubbornly and vowed not to utter another word as the truck bounced over the rough road. She held onto the dash and wished futilely that she'd never gotten in with him. The truck sped down the road through the driving rain and she felt as though her teeth were being shaken from her head. After a couple of miles she turned to him and, with an angry flip of her head, said indignantly, "If you can't drive any better than this, let me drive. You're hitting every hole in the road."

"No thanks," he sneered, his bearing still relentlessly hard and grim. "I've seen some first-hand examples of your driving. It's surprising you're still in one piece."

The windshield wipers swished back and forth before her eyes as a frustrated anger burned within her chest. She felt as if she were about to explode. He always managed to turn the tables on her and win during their verbal battles, and she could think of no plausible retort. First she'd almost run over him; then he'd passed when she'd been stopped for speeding. Anyone who didn't know her would think she really was a careless driver. Damned if she'd tell him it was the first time in her life she had ever been pulled over by a policeman. He wouldn't believe it if she did tell him.

She gave him a look of pure venom, her green eyes flaming with rage, but she bit back hot angry words, refusing to give him the satisfaction of an answer. Instead she stared out the window at the dreary rainswept countryside, wondering how long she could endure the job.

"That scowl isn't exactly what the well-dressed secretary is wearing these days, Miss Kelly," Jed said, his voice clipped and low, as he parked in front of a neat white farmhouse. "I don't want our personal animosity to interfere with our work! Am I understood?"

"Perfectly," Cindy answered resentfully. As if she weren't professional enough to carry on her work!

"Fine," Jed said, an impassive expression on his face. "This is the Harley place. We'll need Map 106 and two blank contracts."

Jed had walked up to the door through the downpour and knocked. He waited impatiently as she trailed behind him, lugging the portable.

"Mr. Harley?" he asked the elderly man in

bibbed overalls who answered the door. At the old man's nod, Jed held out his hand and said, "I'm Jed McCord and this is my secretary, Miss Kelly. We've come to talk about the new highway that's coming through. May we come in?"

"Yep, come in. Me and Maude's been expecting you fellers. This here road's comin' across us, ain't it?" Mr. Harley asked, as he motioned them to a wine-colored sofa in the living room. Cindy let the men talk as she gazed around appreciatively at the homey room. The furniture was old fashioned, but looked nice, as if it had been well taken care of. The shining old tables covered with stiffly starched ruffled doilies held pictures of the Harley family, Cindy surmised. Pictures of children, probably grandchildren, were proudly displayed along with older pictures of two young men in uniform.

Just as Cindy was guessing who the men in the photos might be, a tiny gray-haired lady stepped into the room, drying her hands on a dish towel. "Why didn't you tell me we had company, Dad? Why, these young people have been out in the wet. Would you like a cup of hot coffee, or some cookies? I just took them out of the oven. I always bake cookies when the weather is bad and Dad can't work in the fields." She smiled fondly at her husband and Cindy could see the love between them. It radiated as they talked to each other, and it filled their home.

Wistfully she found herself wishing for a relationship like theirs, one that would endure the years and still be strong. Some day, she promised herself, she would find the right man, one she could spend the rest of her life with.

She smiled warmly at the woman named Maude

and said, "I'd love some coffee, and the cookies smell heavenly. Could I help you with anything?"

"No, no, I'll just be a minute, and the men may need you, dear." With that, Maude bustled cheerfully off to the kitchen and Cindy turned her attention back to the men. Jed was explaining where the road would cross the Harley farm and she could see that Mr. Harley was impressed by his sincere, candid views on the road project. Cindy was surprised at the warm way Jed had of talking to people. Mr. and Mrs. Harley seemed to like him, but she told herself he kept his true obnoxious personality under wraps when he was doing business.

The contracts with the Harleys were signed and, with warm goodbys and promises to come visit again, Jed and Cindy left them waving and dashed through the never-ending rain, back to the truck and the next stop on their list.

They made four more stops and, with each one, Cindy's respect for Jed's natural sincerity increased. She'd just about decided she'd been unfair; maybe if she listened with an open mind, like the people they talked to today, there would be no bad feelings now.

She turned to Jed as he drove the heavy truck with total nonchalance and she knew he'd be just as competent behind the wheel of a smooth-driving car.

"Jed, why did you buy only the right of way from all those people, but insisted on buying my whole place?"

He smiled, and she noticed his even white teeth, and how tanned his face looked. Her use of his first name hadn't escaped him.

"Your house sits right where a rest park goes,"

he explained. "So we decided we had to buy it. Just think of all the people who will enjoy the view after the road goes through."

"Yes, I suppose you're right. But it's a shame to destroy that little house; it's been there a long time." Cindy's tone was still resentful.

Jed gave her a cold look. "I suppose you think the whole road project should have been shelved just because of one rundown little shack stuck up on a hill! How many highways would go in if crazy women like you had their way? And where would you drive that little white sports car of yours if there were no roads?"

"I never said I was against highways, but a person's home is more important than a road." They were back where they'd started, at each other's throats again.

"I've said it once and I'll say it again," Jed stated grimly. "You are without a doubt the most bull-headed woman I've ever had the misfortune to meet."

"And you are an arrogant bully! Furthermore, I don't intend to argue with you. So let's just get on to the next place; I don't want to have to put up with your nasty remarks any longer than necessary." She turned her face to the far window, wishing she were anywhere but there, trapped inside a truck with anger and resentment growing thicker between them.

Jed examined her sulky face and a wry smile flitted on his firm mouth. "Does the truth hurt?" He asked it mildly as he pulled the truck to the side of the road and parked.

Now what? Cindy wondered, as she looked out at the bare expanse of the road. There wasn't a house in sight. Suspiciously she glared at Jed.

"Why are we stopping here? No one lives within miles of this place. I thought we came out here to take care of some contracts."

"Relax, Spitfire," he drawled smoothly, as he turned in the seat to face her. "Your virtue is safe with me. After all, I wouldn't want Pine Valley's most prominent attorney after my hide, would I?" There was a trace of satisfaction in his eyes as he nonchalantly reached into his shirt pocket and withdrew a cigarette. Flicking a long wooden match with his thumbnail, he lit the cigarette and deposited the matchstick in the ashtray next to his knee.

Cindy watched him from beneath lowered lashes, the bold handsome lines of his profile under the shock of black hair coming as a surprise. She grudgingly admitted that he was really quite handsome in a careless sort of way. He didn't have the studied good looks of Brent; no, his face was rugged and he was definitely an outdoors man. Strange that she hadn't noticed before, but she'd been so busy fighting with him that she hadn't realized how attractive he was.

The heavy rain pounded on the cab of the truck, and for a breathless moment Cindy found herself wishing he would take her in his arms. Her heart was racing at his nearness and she willed away the feelings surging through her. She drew a deep breath, trying to still the trembling of her body as she fiddled with the button on her jacket.

Jed smiled crookedly as he reached out a strong hand and loosened the shining copper curls at her neck, allowing them to flow around her shoulders. The hand at her neck came up to cup her chin as he gazed into her eyes. Provocatively she touched her red lips with the tip of her tongue as her breast rose and fell seductively with every breath.

Jed's dark head bent slowly to her and she awaited his kiss . . . but the expected caress never came. Opening her wide green eyes, she saw Jed watching her with sardonic satisfaction.

"I think you do need protecting, Spitfire!" He grinned mockingly. "From yourself!"

Wounded pride and anger boiled to the surface, and as she gazed up at him her eyes swam with hot tears. For the first time she realized he had the power to hurt her, and she hadn't even realized why. *He* was the reason she'd been so restless and felt so alone! With shock she stared at his hard features, and her eyes mirrored her pain, humiliated at the sudden knowledge that she loved him.

The discovery served to deepen her railing emotions, because with it came self-loathing. Never, she vowed, would he know of her feelings—not he or anyone else. He regarded her as a hot-tempered shrew and she'd never give him the satisfaction of knowing she felt anything but contempt for him.

Drawing back a slender hand, she lashed out at him, and all her crashing turmoil exploded with the force of the blow. Numbly she watched as his jaw whitened and then turned red from the sting of her hand.

She forced a defiance she didn't feel as she awaited retaliation for the blow. His face grew dark with rage and his granite jaw tightened as he gripped her shoulders violently. Cindy was trembling. She'd never seen a man so angry before.

"Let me go!" she cried with fear in her voice. "Let go! You're hurting me!"

"You're lucky I don't do more!" Jed told her coldly. "You deserve a sound spanking." As she tried to wrest her arms from his grasp, he shook her roughly. "Keep acting like a spoiled brat and I will," he promised threateningly.

A tear slipped down her cheek and, with a choked sob, she groped for the door handle behind her. As the door sprang open, she jerked from his hold and fled from the truck into the cold driving rain.

She heard his shout as he jumped from the truck and came after her. "You're working for me!" he yelled as he caught up with her. "And as long as you work for me, you'll do your job, understand? Now get that typewriter and follow me."

The cold rain poured down on them as they stood glaring at each other, his hard gray eyes locked with her stormy green ones. But there was no sign of softening on his part and Cindy was too stubborn to give in. Water plastered her hair to her head and she was aware of the sight she must present. The once lovely suit dragged the road at the hems and the brightly colored scarf of which she'd been so proud hung limply around her neck, but the battle of wills raged on.

Drops of rain gleamed in his dark hair and ran down the side of his rugged face. Water dripped off his nose and, as mad as he was, Cindy expected the water to turn to steam. Suddenly she wondered what would happen if someone came by and saw them. She could just hear the whispers in town. "They were standing in the middle of the road, in a downpour of rain, staring at each other. City folks don't have sense enough to come in out of the rain!" Then the humorous aspect of the situation struck her and Jed was bewildered as the fierce look in Cindy's green eyes slowly turned to mirth. To his astonishment, she burst out laughing.

"I swear to heaven," Jed exclaimed, "what's so funny?"

"You," Cindy giggled, "and me too. Do you know what Pine Valley folks would say if they could see us now? They don't think people from the cities are too bright anyway, and look at us."

"Well, you do look like a drowned rat," Jed laughed, pushing a strand of wet red hair away from her face.

"You don't look so hot yourself," Cindy retorted as she pulled the hem of her jacket up and wrung the water out of it. "My suit is ruined," she lamented, smiling still. "Why did you stop here? There's no place around here to talk to anyone. No houses or anything."

"See that path?" Jed pointed to the edge of the road. "The Larkins live about a half mile away. They're on our agenda."

"A half mile up there?" Cindy was incredulous. "Why would they live all the way up there? Without a road, do they walk in and out?"

"Why does anyone want to live away from cities and people?" Jed asked, watching her with keen eyes.

"That's different!" Cindy replied. "At least I had a road up to the house."

"You forget you're in southern Kentucky," Jed reminded her. "These people are descendants of the first settlers. They're strong, independent and self-sufficient. They live up there because that's how they want to live. A half mile to them is no more than a city block to you. You're merely playing at living down here, Spitfire. What would you do if you really had to live here instead of taking a return-to-nature trip?"

"Let's get the typewriter and get going, then!" Cindy said, determined to show him she was stronger than he thought.

"I must admit as I look at you standing here in the middle of the road in this freezing rain, with that bullheaded look on your face, I wonder if you might have just a little of that pioneer stock in you," Jed said. And Cindy detected a twinge of admiration in his voice. "Now let's get out of this weather and go do our job."

TEN

Jed and Cindy slogged through the muddy path beside the road. Both of them were wet and bedraggled because the rain continued to pour from the gray skies, showing no promise of quitting.

Jed fished a pack of wet cigarettes from his jacket pocket and, with a harsh exclamation of disgust, dropped the soggy mass into the litter bag hanging from the knob of the radio. Then he reached past Cindy to grope in the glove box for a dry package.

"It's twelve-thirty," he said as he glanced at his watch. "Your old place is up the road about five miles and I have some food packed for lunch. Want to go up there, build a fire, and dry out before we finish our contract calls?"

"Yes, let's do," Cindy replied, trembling with cold. "I'm about to freeze! I left a few things up there; we were going to move them this weekend. If I'm lucky I'll even find some dry clothes."

A short time later they crossed the bridge at the end of the lane and drove up the hill to the forlorn little cabin. The water running off the steep hill had cut deep gullies in the narrow drive and the truck jiggled and bounced as Jed drove up to the house.

"This road is nearly impassable," he said soberly as he maneuvered the heavy truck around the potholes. "If it's this bad here, there's no telling what's going on out where the new road construction has started. I hope there are no landslides. This damn rain could set us back about three months' work."

"It doesn't look as if it's going to quit for awhile," Cindy said, as she peered out at the dark sky.

"Well, we can't do anything about the weather," Jed told her as he parked in front of the cabin. "So let's get a fire going and dry ourselves out."

Soon Cindy was sorting through a box of clothes she'd left at the house, while Jed gathered some kindling and dry wood that had been stacked on the porch and began building a fire.

"Thank heavens I found a pair of old jeans," she exclaimed to Jed, who was coaxing the fire on the other side of the room. Then her face fell. "But I don't have anything you can put on!"

"Don't worry about me; these jeans will be dry before you know it." Jed smiled at her concern. "You get over here right now and change."

"Here?" she stared blankly at him, apprehension on her face.

"Why do you persist in thinking the worst of me?" Jed ground the words out and added, "If I were half the monster you think I am, I would have ravaged you before now!" With a scowl on his face, he slammed out the door into a windy gust of rain.

Cindy turned to watch his departure, bewildered. She wondered what she had said to light Jed McCord's short fuse. Every time she

125

opened her mouth he sizzled and exploded.

By the time Jed returned, Cindy had slipped out of her wet clothes and was dressed in the old faded jeans and a green checked shirt. She was sitting on the floor combing the tangles from her long red hair. The flickering flames of the fire reflected in the burnished copper hair, and her skin glowed. She felt the veiled alertness of his gaze as she sat there with her feet tucked under her. Darting a timid smile of apology, she lifted the shining mass of hair to the top of her head and pinned it.

Suddenly Jed's gray eyes narrowed and Cindy realized the cotton blouse was very thin. With her arms up her small firm breasts were clearly outlined in the glow from the fire. Flustered, she dropped her arms and blushed crimson. From under lowered lashes she studied the floor intently while she tried to recover her composure.

Calmly Jed walked over and dropped a cooler on the floor at her side. "Lunch," he said shortly.

"Mr. McCord . . . Jed," Cindy began hesitantly, "I'm sorry. I didn't mean to make you angry. It seems we can't manage a conversation without fighting. Let's forget lunch and get back to work. The sooner we finish our calls the quicker we can get away from each other."

"It doesn't look as if we'll be parting company for awhile, Spitfire," he answered as he dropped down on the floor before the fire. "There's been a slide down at the end of the drive and it doesn't look good."

"A slide?" Cindy's voice was disbelieving as she stared at him with an incredulous expression. "A rock slide on my drive!"

"You can go look if you like. It's not a rock slide, it's mud. I was worried about that happening at the road site but I never thought it would happen here. I doubt if the truck can get through." Jed shrugged.

"We'll just have to walk back to town!" Cindy exclaimed. "We can't stay here, you know. No one has any idea where we are."

"Are you prepared to wade through four feet of mud in a pouring rain, to say nothing of walking seven miles into town in those shoes?" Jed's tone was contemptuous as he glared at her. "Go right ahead, but don't expect me to follow you. I'm staying right here, at least until it quits raining."

Worriedly, Cindy got up from the floor and went to the window, where she looked out at the bleak dismal weather. The window had misted over a little with steam and she rubbed it so she could see the damage at the end of the drive, but the blowing rain blocked her view. She turned back to Jed, disheartened. "I guess we'll have to stay here until someone comes to clear the road. But what if we have to spend the night? There are no beds here. Where will we sleep?"

"I have a sleeping bag in the truck which I use when I go fishing. But maybe we'll be lucky and someone will come along before night falls. Now let's eat."

"I suppose you're right. One of the neighbors from up the road will come by and see what's happened," Cindy reassured herself, and she sat down before the fire. "We'll have an inside picnic today." She was doing her best to look at the bright side of things, knowing she must keep up a pretense at enjoyment or start crying.

The idea of spending the night with Jed was frightening. After the feelings she'd discovered this afternoon, she knew she would have to keep her distance from him. She'd die before she'd admit it, but he'd been right. She did need protection—from him, and herself.

Cindy had never had any doubt about her self-control before, not even with Brent. But now she was faced with feelings she'd never experienced for a man. Quick hot flashes of desire had surged through her when he'd held her in his arms. The warm rush of pleasure that filled her when he smiled at her came unbidden to mind, intermingled with the dark despairing knowledge that he didn't return the feeling she had for him.

She remembered his cold statement to her that day in the barn, when he referred to women as mere momentary pleasures, and she knew he'd never be the kind to settle down. Cindy prayed she'd be able to keep him from knowing how she felt. It would only add to his arrogance to know she'd succumbed to his attractions. Damned if she'd be just another woman who gave him pleasure for the moment.

"If you're not careful you'll chew that lip off!" The humor in Jed's voice made her realize he'd been watching her for some time. As she raised her eyes to his, she caught the bold speculation in his gaze. "Are you afraid to spend the day and maybe the night with me?" he taunted.

"Why should I be afraid?" Cindy's voice was steady, hiding the quaking of her insides. She hoped he hadn't guessed how she felt and wondered why he watched her so closely. Well, she would never confirm his suspicions. Without being aware of it, Cindy tilted her chin stubbornly and vowed she'd not be another in his long line of conquests.

"You've made up your mind about something,"

Jed said idly, but his eyes were keen as he watched her. It was as if he'd read her mind. Under his penetrating gaze Cindy shifted uneasily, but refused to divulge her churning thoughts.

"Well, are you going to enlighten me?" Jed asked, his dark eyes glinting.

"About what?" Cindy hedged, stalling for time while she tried to put her mind and emotions in order. But with his eyes on her, it was proving difficult.

"Don't beat around the bush. I can tell from the set of your chin and the determination in those emerald eyes that you've made a decision, and it doesn't look as if you'll be swayed from it. Now 'fess up, what have you got in your head this time?"

Cindy was beginning to wonder if he could read her mind. His clear gray eyes reminded her of a show she had seen where a hypnotist exerted power over his victim. She poked at the crackling fire. Evading his hard gaze, she replied, "I suppose I'll have to stay here, at least until someone comes. But I won't stay for one minute if you get out of line. You must promise to keep your hands to yourself, and if we do have to spend the night together, we sleep apart. Is that clear?"

"You overestimate your charms, *Miss Kelly*. I think I told you before, you're not my kind of woman!" Jed's harsh voice tore into her. "You can consider yourself safe with me, now and always."

With pain gnawing at her insides, Cindy forced a calmness to her voice as she said, "Thank you, Mr. McCord. That's exactly what I wanted to hear."

"Now if you'll excuse me, I think I'll see if I can hear any news on the truck radio." His jaw was granite hard and anger simmered in his eyes.

"But . . . but what about the food . . . ." Cindy stammered, waving her hand distractedly at the cooler.

"I believe something just killed my appetite," Jed sneered as he crossed the room with long angry strides. At the door he turned, and the cold glare he gave her sent a chill through her. "You're as barren as this room, and you were right: you should have been allowed to keep this place. That way you could hide from life forever. You came down here with a rosy picture of yourself living here on the hill like a princess, removed from the harsher aspects of reality. You've somehow gotten the idea that a line has been drawn between the city and the country, that everything is black in the city and white in the country. Real life doesn't work that way, and the sooner you face up to it the better off you'll be."

Numbly Cindy turned away, his bitter words like a slap in the face. He was right: she had been hiding from life when she'd left Lexington and moved to this little cabin. The episode with Brent had been her excuse to withdraw into her childhood fantasy of country living.

Once she had said it didn't matter where you lived so long as it was with someone you loved. And she'd been right. This cabin, the city, anywhere would be fine if only she could be with Jed. But it would never happen, and she took small comfort in the knowledge that she'd grown up enough in the last few hours to know he wasn't interested in a permanent relationship.

After a few minutes Cindy walked to the window and looked out, hoping she'd see some activity at the end of the drive. If there was, then she'd know someone was trying to clear the road. But as she stared at the road her hopes of being rescued dwindled. The neighbors knew she'd moved to town, so even if they noticed the mud slide they wouldn't try to clear it off or report it to the authorities. They had no way of knowing anyone was trapped in the old cabin.

Disheartened, she glanced down at the watch on her slender wrist. Three-thirty and the rain was still pelting the earth as furiously as ever. The glowering sky made it seem later than it really was and Cindy knew the days were a lot shorter now. If it didn't stop raining before long it would be too dark to try to walk out for help. Then it would be a certainty they would have to spend the night together.

The shadows in the small room lengthened as the day grew shorter. At a quarter past five Jed hadn't returned. Cindy paced the floor, back and forth between the fireplace and the window. She lost all hope of help coming to clear the drive and the approaching night completely unnerved her. She interrupted her tense pacing and poked another stick of wood on the fire. Red and yellow sparks flickered from the glowing red coals. There wasn't much dry wood left, she noticed, certainly not enough to last the night, and the wind was beginning to howl as the gale increased. She wondered how they would keep warm.

The quiet serenity of the house was no longer inviting. She wished she were at home with her parents. A nervous giggle escaped her as she realized Jed had been right; when things got a little rough she was ready to run away. A fit of sneezing interrupted her jittery musings. On top of everything else, she didn't need to come down with a stupid cold.

"Get over next to the fire. You're taking a cold, Miss Kelly." Jed's impassive expression as he stood there, holding a large sleeping bag, filled her with renewed anxieties.

"What did the radio say?" she asked, her eyes grave. "Is it going to quit raining before long?"

"No chance of its letting up until morning. Flash flood warnings out for the southern part of the state, so it looks as if we're going to have to put up with each other until daybreak, maybe longer." All signs of Jed's previous bad temper had been erased as he smiled mockingly at her. "Now if you'll quit picking quarrels, we might manage to get through the night without killing one another."

"Me! I didn't start anything," Cindy cried indignantly. "You're so blasted arrogant you think . . . aaaah . . . choo . . . . "

Jed's eyes crinkled with amusement and to Cindy's chagrin he burst out laughing.

"Oh, shut up!" she muttered, turning her back on his flashing smile.

Firmly Jed propelled her over to the fireplace. "You'd better stay by the heat," he ordered crisply. "You're a stubborn little fool but there's no sense in making matters worse by risking pneumonia."

At the touch of his hands Cindy trembled, tensing against the warm rush of desire that came unbidden.

Abruptly Jed's expression softened. "You're cold and shaking. Come here."

Cindy was surprised at the gentleness of his embrace when his strong arms pulled her close to the warmth of his lean body. Large hands tenderly smoothed her hair and she released the tight hold

132

on her emotions and surrendered to the comforting strength of his arms.

"I hope you realize I can't stand here and hold you like this much longer." Jed's body was suddenly tense.

Cindy could feel the steady beat of his heart as she pressed closer to his lean male length. She knew she was playing with fire but she resisted the idea of pulling away. A slow languor was invading her body and she could not resist a glance up at him. Dreamily she watched the firelight play across his face and glint on his thick dark hair. His gray eyes were questioning as he gazed down at her eyes.

"A man could drown in those emerald eyes," he whispered as he bent close to her lips.

Unaware of what she was doing, Cindy raised her parted lips to his kiss and a terrifying sweetness engulfed her. The room seemed to whirl and plummet all at the same moment. Her hands touched his hard chest and slipped up around his neck as she lifted her face hungrily for his kiss. She could feel her heart thudding, and his, too.

Jed raised his head and his lazy gray eyes roamed over her face, drinking in the longing he saw there. Slowly he raised his hands to the pins holding her bright coppery hair, never taking his gaze from her face. One by one he dropped the pins on the floor, allowing the burnished strands to cascade in shimmering waves and curls on her shoulders. With agonizing slowness his fingers moved with practiced skill to the buttons of her thin shirt. The blouse fell to the floor with the discarded pins.

Jed's gray eyes darkened as she stood before him in all her glorious disarray. His hands slipped over her satiny skin to the rosy peaks of her small firm breasts. A flame flickered in the lower part of her body and slowly burned through her. A moan slipped from her lips as, deep in the recesses of her mind, a voice told her to stop. But her body refused to listen to the dictates of her brain.

"Lord, you're beautiful, Spitfire," he whispered, as he pulled her against the hardness of his aroused male passion. His lips were trailing flames of searing sensations as his lips traveled down the slender white column of her throat and his dark head bent to the lush curves below.

She trembled under the force of his passion as her body curved up to meet his with mounting excitement. Wild abandonment surged through her and she clung to him, drowning in a vortex of burning desire.

Jed's fingers twisted in a tangle of red curls at her neck and he held her in a ruthless grip as he stared down at her. "You want me, don't you?" he muttered as he watched her with hard eyes. "Tell me you want me!"

Wordlessly she nodded, as emotions she'd never before experienced soared through her. Her lips parted seductively and her breasts rose, swollen with desire.

"Have you made love before?" Jed asked, his voice harsh.

Cindy's eyes widened as his question soaked into her bemused state, and surprise at his harsh attitude left her speechless. Shame flooded her body and she flinched as though he'd struck her. He was asking her if she was experienced!

The words he had spoken to her before returned to haunt her. He was reminding her he was interested in experienced women only, those momentary pleasures in his life that she had been thinking about only moments before.

In that split second she made her decision. She loved him and, even though she knew he would never return that love, she wanted a taste of heaven now that it was within her grasp. All right, she would be one of his momentary pleasures; for one burning interlude she would throw her pride to the winds.

"Answer me, damn you," he commanded her.

"Of course I have," she lied softly, hiding her innocence beneath a curling sweep of lashes.

An icy fury crossed his face for a second, before an impenetrable mask dropped over his features. With his hands still locked in her wild tangle of hair, his mouth crushed down on hers savagely. His hard lips ground against hers and she could taste blood. His embrace was cruel and punishing and she moaned against the pain of his brutal hold. He held her in a vicelike grip as his hands roamed over her slender body, causing the creamy skin to redden under his rough treatment.

What had started out to be ecstasy had turned into a nightmare and she fought him with all her strength.

"You're *hurting* me," she cried, trying to free himself from his iron grasp.

"I intend to," Jed retorted coldly, as rage distorted his dark features. "Tell me, who was it? That weak mama's boy, the lawyer? Or have there been others?" His fingers tightened cruelly as he shook her so hard her hair whipped across his face.

Wrenching an arm free, Cindy's hand flashed and her nails plowed a red furrow down the side of his granite jaw. Her green eyes were dark with a spitting fury as she stood slim and proud before him. Her bare chest heaved and she spat contemptuously, "It's none of your damn business who it was!"

"You'll tell me." The quiet tone of his voice was ominous as he started toward her, ignoring the thin trickle of blood on his face. Fear invaded her as he approached.

"You said you were only interested in women with experience," she whispered as she backed away from him. Her lips quivered and she swallowed as she dashed angrily at the glitter of tears on her cheek. *Well, I'm not experienced, and I don't want to be, either!* If all men are like you then they can stay away from me."

Jed hesitated, an unconvinced expression on his face. "You were lying?" His eyes searched her tearstained face and softly, almost to himself, he said, "I should have known. Your innocence is plain to see."

He raised his hand as if to touch her cheek and she drew away sharply. *"Don't ever touch me again!* I loathe and despise you and if I ever get away from here, I never want to see you again!"

She pulled the shredded remnants of her pride around her and bent to retrieve the discarded shirt from the floor. Shame and self-contempt raged in her heart and she fumbled with the buttons with stiff, trembling fingers.

Jed watched her unsteady progress for awhile. Then, with an ironic expression, he brushed her shaking hands aside, his expression revealing nothing as he fastened the little white buttons.

She tensed, poised like a startled deer, her eyes wide and fearful.

"Stop looking at me like that!" His tone was

harsh. "I won't touch you again."

Cindy pulled away from him and turned to the window. She rested her hot forehead against the cold damp glass and wished for a place to lay her aching head and cry. The high, dizzying peaks of emotion had left her shaking, and weariness washed over her. She reeled with dizziness and had to clutch the window sash and hang on until the room righted itself.

Jed watched her intently as she crossed over to the fireplace, but he made no comment as she sat before the fire and drew her knees up to rest her head on them. Her tousled curls fell forward and covered her flushed face, blocking it from Jed's view.

The silence of the dark cabin was broken only by the shrieking wind, the crackling of the fire, and the steady hammering of the rain on the roof. Cindy shifted her cramped position and stretched her long slender legs, leaned against the hard wall and tried to sleep. The bright flare of a match disturbed her and with resentment she watched the red glow of his cigarette in the darkness. Nothing seemed to ruffle his stoic exterior and she was beginning to wonder if anything ever would.

Her head was pounding and she blamed it on her awkward position as she tiredly rubbed the back of her neck and wished for the night to end. Suddenly a dark figure loomed out of the darkness and dropped an object beside her.

"Here." Jed's voice came from the darkness. "Try to get some sleep. We're running out of wood and it's going to get cold, damned cold."

The large sleeping bag lay at her feet and she wanted nothing more at that moment than to climb into it and sleep her miseries away, but her stubborn pride forced her to refuse.

"It's yours, you use it!"

"I said take it," Jed commanded, "and I won't take no for an answer."

"No!" she said mulishly. "I won't take it. I won't sleep in it and you can't make me."

"You are absolutely the most hardheaded woman I've ever met. If you don't get into this sleeping bag, I'll put you in it!" His voice had taken on a dangerous edge and, in spite of herself, she shivered.

"No!" All the frustrations of the day focused on her decision and she was determined not to give in.

"This is your last chance," he said coldly. Although she couldn't see his face, his anger was a tangible force.

"I will not!" she stated firmly, folding her arms across her chest.

The words had hardly let her mouth before she was seized by the shoulders and hauled firmly to her feet. With surprising agility for a man so tall, he flipped her around and with one arm held her firmly against him while he plucked the bag from the floor.

She was furious. Blood pounded in her head as she struggled and kicked. If only she could turn in his grasp, she'd scratch his eyes out. She flailed the air behind her and managed to get one hand in his hair. Using every bit of her strength, she pulled with all her might.

Jed had to drop the bag as he pried her fingers from his hair; then he pulled her arm down to her side. With both his arms around her, he lifted her wildly kicking feet from the floor and shook her up and down.

So far this had been a silent struggle punctuated only by groans, moans and a lot of loud panting. But Jed broke the silence when he asked, "Now are you going to get in that bag?"

"Yes," she replied softly, "I will . . . when hell freezes over!"

Jed had relaxed his hold at her soft tone and he was taken by surprise as she turned, swift as a cat in his arms, and plowed him one right in the jaw with her small fist.

It hurt her worse than it did him, but it held the element of surprise and, before he could get a hold on her, she grabbed his ear and yanked hard.

With less than gentle hands, he once again pried her fingers loose and held her tightly against him. Her feet drummed on his shins and as he stepped back to get away from them, his own feet tangled in the sleeping bag and they both fell to the floor in a heap. He rolled around and managed to wrap his legs around her squirming body. He held her that way until he could get the bag straightened out, then he poked her thrashing legs into the bag and worked it up over her body until the only part of her that remained free was her head. Her strength had failed and she was where he'd promised she'd be, but she had the satisfaction of knowing it hadn't been easy for him.

"Now are you going to settle down and behave?" He was gasping for breath. "If I have to I'll hold you here all night."

"I wish I were a man," she choked bitterly. "Then you'd be the one in this bag! You're contemptible, using brute strength on a defenseless woman!"

"Defenseless, hell!" Jed snorted and a trace of rueful amusement entered his voice. "I was fighting for my life!"

"You started the quarrel," she answered stiffly. "I will not be dictated to any more. I let one man treat me that way, but never again."

"I'd like to meet the man who ruled you, Spitfire." Jed laughed unbelievingly. "It wasn't Arthur Corry, was it?"

"Go away." She refused to tell him any of the facts of her life and she wasn't going to listen to him put Arthur down again, either.

"No, it wasn't Arthur. I've seen you two together," he mused. "You rule him."

A smile curved her full lips in the darkness. She had him puzzled and she intended to keep him that way. "Why are you so interested? Arthur isn't the only man in the world."

"Maybe not, but he's the one you've turned your feminine wiles on, isn't he? The poor devil. I pity him when he finds out just how bad-tempered you really are. He's too soft. He'll never be able to handle you. You need a real man."

"I suppose you're referring to yourself," she snapped.

"I could handle you, Spitfire. And I must admit it would be a challenge, and I'm positive it wouldn't be boring."

"Don't get any ideas, you arrogant worm. I wouldn't have you if you were the last man on earth." Her scornful tones rang in the small room. "I don't think I've ever met anyone as low as you!"

"You didn't act that way a few hours ago," he taunted mockingly, "But your virtue is safe. I've better things to do than to waste my time on you!"

The hurt slammed into her as his words reinforced her convictions of the way he felt. She'd never let him know she cared for him, she promised herself, as she fought back the tears. "Leave me alone! Go away!" Her words sounded childish, but she didn't care.

As he shifted his weight and stood up, her heart cried out for him to stay and hold her, but she stayed in silence where he had left her, listening as he crossed the room. Tears rolled down her cheeks and she muffled her face in the downfilled bag to keep him from suspecting he'd made her cry again.

ELEVEN

She awakened to the gray light of dawn. A dark lethargy dulled her senses and for a few moments she couldn't remember where she was. Her body felt bruised and battered and then she shuddered violently as memories of the night before came back to her.

She crawled out of the sleeping bag and her sore muscles protested painfully. When she stood up gingerly her legs shook. Jed was nowhere to be seen, for that she was thankful.

"Let's get out of here!" His harsh voice caused her to jump. She turned to the kitchen door and her green eyes widened when she saw the long red scratch running down the side of his granite-hard face. She swallowed and dropped her gaze.

Without a word she followed him out to the truck. His closed expression and his silence forestalled any attempt on her part to make conversation. She'd watched him furtively as he drove down the hill and, with a sinking heart, she realized how anxious he was to be rid of her. From the window of the truck she gazed at the terrible destruction the storm had wrought.

The damage to the road was worse than she'd imagined and she knew the truck would never get through the mass of mud, uprooted saplings and stones.

A strange noise from the creek filtered into her consciousness and as she stepped out of the truck she gasped. The normally placid creek she'd bathed in had turned into a wide muddy river, fed by the small branches and gullies that cut down the hill, and the small stream had overflowed its banks. Dirty water lapped at the trees at the edge of the woods. Even as she watched it, it climbed higher, the surface covered with floating objects that had been swallowed up and hurled along with the rushing floodwaters. It would be a long time before the full extent of the damage could be assessed.

The sound of a horn over on the highway brought her eyes away from the distressing sight below. With glad relief she recognized Jan's bright yellow Volkswagen.

She climbed on a large boulder beside the road and waved to catch Jan's attention.

"We're coming over," she called across the distance. The wind blew her copper curls and molded the thin blouse to her body. As she jumped from the rock she saw Jed watching her.

His brooding eyes and grim expression forced her to assume an indifferent attitude as she picked her way below the slide area to get across to Jan. She could hear his footsteps behind her but she didn't dare turn for fear of showing him the despair in her eyes. His silence was tearing her to pieces as she trudged up the rough hill, and by the time they'd reached the top her chin was quivering and she was afraid she'd lose control. Not daring to risk a glance at Jed, she hurried the last few steps to Jan's car.

"How in the world did you get out here?" Jan's anxiety hung around her like a cloud. "This was the only place I could think to look for you! Are you all right?" This last was directed to Cindy as Jan's glance took in Jed's grim countenance and the long scratch on his jaw.

"We're fine, Jan."

"Well, if you say so." But Jan's glance was doubtful as her eyes traveled from Cindy's bleak expression to Jed's hard impassive features. Holding back curious questions—which, for the garrulous Jan, showed remarkable restraint—she motioned to the small car. "Hop in and I'll have you back to town in no time."

Cindy climbed into the back seat of the car and Jed wedged his tall frame into the front. She was glad she didn't have to ride all the way to town with his cold eyes boring into her back. This way she could see his profile when he looked at Jan or out the window, although that was small comfort. After today their relationship would be purely business. Biting her lip, she stared unseeingly out the side window.

"Arthur has been so worried about you, Cindy," Jan said as she shifted gears. "Did you forget you were supposed to meet his mother last night?"

"I did," she admitted slowly. "I'm sorry. I'll call and apologize as soon as I get home." Darting a glance at Jed's profile, she noticed that his jaw had tightened perceptibly. He doesn't approve of anything I do, she thought hopelessly. All he wants is to get me off his hands.

"Millie will appreciate that, Cindy, but I'm sure she'll understand why you couldn't make it. Oh yes, the storm has done incredible damage. I almost forgot, guess who else is in town?"

"Who?" Cindy asked listlessly, as she watched the passing scenery.

"Your fiance, that's who!" Jan said, watching her reaction in the rear-view mirror.

"Brent? Brent's in town?" Cindy was speechless with shock. She couldn't imagine why he had come. Her mind reeled under the news. Questions formed on her lips, but she knew she would have to see Brent to have them answered. After their last meeting she'd thought she'd never see him again, but he had come. He was in Pine Valley. She was amazed at his having the nerve to face her after their last meeting.

Jan drove down to the end of Main Street and parked in front of the McCord Construction field office. Jed stepped out and closed the door firmly. Leaning down to the window, he said, "Thank you for the lift, Miss Jenkins." Then, with a dry cynicism, he nodded toward the back and added, "Take our Miss Kelly home so she can make herself beautiful. It's not often a woman has a chance to introduce her fiance to her boyfriend." His eyes were smoldering as he nodded curtly and strode away.

"What got into him?" Jan's eyes were huge. "Was it something I said? What happened out at the cabin? I saw that scratch! Did you have to fight him off?" She'd held back for as long as she could and now the questions tumbled from her lips.

"No, it wasn't you, Jan," Cindy replied, holding back bitter tears. "It's me! Take me home, and on the way I'll tell you all about it."

"So you see," Cindy finished her story as the little car stopped in the drive of their new home, "I've fallen in love with him, he doesn't want me, and now Brent is here and I'm so confused . . . ."

Her voice trailed off, and with a sob she dashed to the house.

Jan sighed helplessly as she followed Cindy to the door. As they entered the house, Jan gestured toward the bathroom. "Go take a hot bath and I'll fix you something to eat. Things will look a lot better after you get some warm food in you." Jan had faith in the restorative powers of food and her chunky little figure reflected it. Although she couldn't solve Cindy's problems, she could alleviate them for the time being.

Moments later, Cindy came out of the bathroom dressed in a warm terry cloth robe. A large towel was twisted turban style around her wet head and she gratefully sank into a chair to enjoy the steaming coffee Jan placed before her.

Her emerald eyes were enormous in her pale face. Although she'd regained her composure, the long hours spent out at the cabin had changed her perspective. All her preconceived ideas of the simplicity of the country had changed. Now she knew life wasn't any different, city or country, and there would be problems no matter where she lived.

"You were right, Jan." She smiled, but only with her lips. Her eyes retained the pain that darkened the iris and made them appear almost brown. "A warm bath and hot coffee can cure almost anything."

"Oh, Cindy, I'm glad you're feeling better. I had some news I wanted to tell you." Jan's face reflected a deep joy and, as Cindy gazed at her friend, she could guess what the news was going to be.

"Hank proposed," she exclaimed, forgetting her own troubles as a smile flitted at the corners of her mouth.

"Yes, he did!" Jan was ecstatic. "Last night. We were both worried about you and when he proposed I couldn't believe my ears. He said he wanted to take care of me; he didn't want ever to have to worry about me being missing. But he kept telling me he knew you were safe."

"Jan, I'm so happy for you." Cindy laughed shakily. "At least my night helped you, and I'm glad. When is the wedding? Will I be hunting a new home again?"

"We've set the date for June. I've always wanted to be a June bride. Will you be my bridesmaid?" Jan was bubbling, and it was infectious. Cindy shoved all her troubled thoughts behind her and her good feeling for Jan chased away the dark clouds that hovered in her mind.

"Of course I'll be your bridesmaid. Did you think you could get married without me at your side?" Warmly she regarded the happy face of her friend, thankful that Hank had overcome his reservations.

"Oh gosh, I've got to get to work!" Jan exclaimed. "I told them I'd be late but I would be in as soon as we found you. You get some rest and I'll see you tonight." And with that, the irrepressible Jan rushed from the door. Presently Cindy heard the Volkswagen sputter to life and chug out of the drive toward town.

She picked up her coffee and walked through the silent house to the living room. After a few minutes she set the cup beside the phone and curled dejectedly into the overstuffed chair. Memories of Jed's hard gray eyes haunted her, but she reminded herself she still had her pride, and she was glad she hadn't confessed her love for

147

him. She could go to work and hold her head up, and she would do it too. Running away and hiding wasn't the answer, she'd finally realized.

A deep weariness washed over her and she yearned for the soft clean bed upstairs. But before she could allow herself that luxury she had to make the call to Arthur and let him know she was all right. She dialed his office number and asked his receptionist if she might speak to him.

"Cindy!" Arthur's relief was evident. "What happened to you? We were so worried!"

"I was at the cabin and a mud slide blocked the road." Cindy had decided not to tell him Jed was with her unless he asked her. She had an idea he had guessed her feelings for Jed the day they'd had the picnic at the cabin, and she was afraid if she spoke of Jed her voice would confirm his suspicions.

"Mother and Sudie were very disappointed that you couldn't make it last night. When we heard about all the damage done by the storm, we knew something had happened to detain you."

"Oh, Arthur, I'm sorry, but I couldn't call. Will you apologize to your mother and Sudie and ask them if we can make it another night? I know they must think I'm terrible!" Cindy was distressed at the thought of the two older ladies waiting and worrying about her last night.

Arthur's calm tones were soothing. "I'm sure they'll just be relieved to know you're all right. Things were bad all over the county last night. I heard that the McCord Construction Company was devastated in the flood. I don't know how many pieces of large equipment were damaged at the road site; the ground gave way and buried them under tons of mud. I would imagine it will set the company back months on its deadlines. This has to be a terrible blow for McCord, although I think he's financially able to absorb the damages. His affluence is known across the state."

Cindy's senses reeled with the news. Jed had good reason for alarm. The road was washed out just as he'd feared. Yet even as they'd fought and argued, he'd known or guessed the problems the rain would cause and he'd never mentioned it. She'd been thoughtless, with all her concern turned toward herself. She berated herself and made up her mind to apologize.

"Cindy? Cindy?" Arthur's voice rang in her ears. "Are you there?"

"Oh . . . yes, I'm here," she answered. "I'm sorry, I guess I lost you for just a moment."

"You hang up the phone and get to bed," Arthur said solicitously. "A good rest will help you more than anything. I'll call you later tonight, all right?"

"Yes, all right," she agreed, letting him believe fatigue was the cause of her vagueness. "And please talk to your mother for me and let me know tonight when we can get together."

"I will," Arthur replied. "Goodby until tonight."

"By," she murmured as she replaced the receiver.

Jed's grim features came into her mind as she contemplated the scene as it must be right now down at the construction office. The emergency situation would call for every able hand to be there. She was tempted to call Ben Kendrick and see if they needed her. No, Jed had sent her home, so if he wanted her help he could call. Her stubborn pride had made the decision but her heart cried for her to go to his side and help him whether he wanted her or not. She hesitated, torn with indecision, her teeth worrying her bottom lip as she wondered what she should do. She picked up the phone, prepared to call the office. But, fearing rejection, she replaced the receiver. Her pride had won.

Tabby wandered in from the kitchen and strutted across the living room carpet with her tail waving. She leaped on Cindy's lap and settled there, purring contentedly. Cindy reached down with a slender finger and tickled her behind a pointed ear. "Pretty Tabby," she crooned. "At least you love me, don't you? Come on, little girl, we'll nap together."

She picked up the calico bundle of fur and started for the stairs. But just as she placed a foot on the first step, the phone rang. She turned back and dashed for the phone, hoping it was Jed saying he needed her.

"Hello." There was a happy lilt in her voice as she waited to hear Jed's deep tones.

"Cindy darling! I've been nearly crazy with worry. Where have you been hiding?" Brent's voice wiped the happy expectancy from her face and disappointment, tinged with impatience, colored her response.

"What makes you think I'd be hiding from you? After our last meeting, I never thought we'd see each other again! Why are you down here?"

"Darling, I hoped by now you'd had time to think and to reconsider your decision. I've come to take you back . . . that is, if you want to go." This he added hastily, as if he realized how arrogant he had sounded.

"Brent," she began evenly, "I returned your ring. I'm not going to change my mind, and I'm not going back to the city with you now or ever."

"Darling, at least meet with me. I've come a long way and I just want to see your gorgeous face one more time. Then, darling, if you're still adamant, I'll go home." Brent's charm oozed, sickening sweet, from the phone.

She couldn't believe him. He was still trying to change her mind. "Brent, don't call me darling! I won't have it. And I won't meet you either. I'll never go through another meeting like our last. You were abusive and vile. And frankly, I'm surprised you have the nerve to ask."

"Cindy, I want to . . . . " His voice trailed off as she firmly replaced the receiver of the phone and turned away. She refused to listen to him any longer and she definitely was not meeting him anywhere.

The phone shrilled again and with an angry look Cindy started to walk away. But on second thought she decided to answer it; it could be Jed.

"Don't hang up." Brent's voice rang out. "You must listen to me. I love you and I know I was terrible the last time we were together. But you must believe me, I'm sorry and I want to make it up to you. My only excuse is I had too much to drink."

"Brent," she said evenly, "it doesn't matter. You don't have to make up for anything. You don't want me, Brent. It's just that your pride has been hurt. You've never been turned down before and you can't accept it."

"You can't believe . . . ."

"Go home, Brent," she said, and hung up.

The telephone rang immediately. "Say you'll see me. I'll keep calling until you do. Just give me one chance to change your mind. If I can't, I'll go home." Brent was begging now and Cindy was too softhearted to hold out against his pleas.

"All right, Brent," she sighed, giving in. "I'll meet you at the motel diner and we'll talk. But I'm not going to change my mind."

"What time will you be here?" he asked eagerly. "Will you make it soon?"

"I can't come until five this afternoon." Her voice was firm enough to dissuade him from pushing her any further.

"I'll see you at five, then. Goodby, darling." The last was a low murmur just before he hung up.

Cindy replaced the phone distastefully, as though it were an extension of the man she'd just been speaking to. It irked her that he expected her to go back with him as though nothing had happened. His unfaithfulness was bad enough, but the terrible words he'd flung at her in the restaurant had widened the breach between them and there was no way it could be mended.

She would have to get some rest now for there was no telling what Brent would do, and she wanted to be at her best when she met him. Still carrying the gently purring cat, she climbed the stairs to her bedroom. She was exhausted and common sense told her Jed wouldn't call her today.

TWELVE

At precisely five o'clock Cindy parked her small white sports car in front of the motel diner. Her sleep had removed most of the dejection and misery, but there was a graveness in her wide green eyes that hadn't been there before—the only outward sign of the changes the night before had wrought.

With misgivings on the wisdom of meeting Brent, she stepped slowly from the car. Dressed in jeans and a blue-and-green-plaid flannel shirt, with her red-gold curls trailing across her slim shoulders, she looked as cool and collected as always. Her reflection in the mirror had surprised her, for she'd felt the change in her would surely affect her appearance. But outwardly she was still the same as before.

"Sweetheart!" Brent's toothy smile made her want to step back into the car and drive away. She felt sure he was prepared to use every trick he knew to persuade her to return to the city. She stood beside the car and watched as he came toward her, his arms outstretched. His self-confident bearing made her wince; she realized he thought he was superior to the people around him, that he was a snob.

And with this understanding came pity. Poor Brent, there was so much in life that he was too blind to see. His high and mighty ways would always separate him from the basic goodness of others, and his opinions would continue to be based on how sophisticated and polished his associates appeared to be. He lived only for an endless round of cocktail parties and hollow laughter. He had come to try to return her to that kind of life, but she was confident that, no matter what happened in Pine Valley, she belonged here.

Standing quietly, she suffered his embrace, and she was relieved to discover that all the bad feelings she'd harbored for Brent over the past months had evaporated. The hurt, the anger and the misguided love had all slipped away, and she was glad he'd come for now she could lay the past to rest.

She waited passively for Brent to release her, her mind clear with the decision. She had to make him understand that any arguments were useless and his trip had been for nothing. As she stood within the circle of his arms, a shadow fell across them. She raised her eyes to see Jed leaning against the iron rail that ran beside the walk of the motel. His gray eyes flicked her with cold contempt as he savagely ground out a half-smoked cigarette beneath his heel.

Embarrassed, she shoved Brent away. "Jed," she said through dry lips, "I . . . I . . . ."

"Miss Kelly." He nodded curtly as he bent to pick up two suitcases she hadn't noticed before. Without another word, he turned and took his familiar swinging strides toward his black truck. Her shoulders sagged with defeat as she watched the truck disappear into the distance.

Cindy's meeting with Brent passed in a blur. Somehow she'd managed to convince him of her determination to stay in Pine Valley, which meant his trip to see her was hopeless. He'd left with a crestfallen expression, but she doubted if many days would pass before he was back in the midst of a bevy of infatuated girls and flashy parties. That would always be Brent's life, but it would never be hers.

The next morning she returned to work with misgivings, with no idea of what to expect. Ben Kendrick flashed her a friendly grin as he turned from unlocking the office door. "Good morning," he said, as he motioned her into the office. "Am I glad to see you!"

"Why?" Cindy asked as she gazed around the room. The desk Jed usually occupied was bare and the office seemed bereft by his absence. All the papers and plat books were missing and she knew before Ben said a word that Jed had left.

"If you'd been here yesterday you wouldn't ask why. I had my hands full." Ben's voice reflected the helplessness he must have felt the day before.

"You should have called me," Cindy said quietly.

"If it were up to me I would have, but Jed vetoed the idea. He said you needed the rest. But let me warn you, now you'll be one busy lady for the next few weeks."

The mere mention of Jed's name brought her attention back to Ben's face. "Where is Mr. McCord?" she asked curiously.

"He's gone back to Lexington. The damage out at the road area has caused more problems than can be handled here. Jed will oversee everything there at the main office and we'll take care of this end. Between the two of us, we'll do all right."

Her first reaction to Ben's announcement was a vast relief, knowing she wouldn't have to face Jed's cold contemptuous gaze. She was afraid she lacked the strength to work with him and face the harsh treatment he'd been prepared to deal out. Although she'd never admit it to Jed, his hard attitude had left a sore spot in her spirits and it would be some time before she would again be able to stand up to his arrogance and fight back.

"Then he won't be down here at all, Mr. Kendrick?" She spoke slowly, as the relief was replaced with a sick emptiness in her stomach. This was his way of severing any connections they might have. He'd maneuvered the job in Pine Valley for her himself, so it would be awkward for him to fire her. By returning to Lexington he'd settled the problem. Her heart plummeted as she realized this was what he'd wanted all along. She'd been a thorn in his side, but since he'd taken her farm he gave her the job to keep her occupied. Everything had been settled in his own ruthless way, and now that he didn't need anything more, he'd gone on to some other business.

She didn't realize her heart was in her eyes as she gazed helplessly at Ben Kendrick. "I guess that takes care of that, Mr. Kendrick," she murmured.

"Call me, Ben, will you?" he asked gruffly as he tried to hide the sympathy that welled up at the sight of her woebegone face. "He'll be dropping in from time to time, but he'll work principally from the Lexington office."

The total devastation of the terrible flood began to dawn on Cindy as reports trickled into the office, accompanied by estimates of the dollar loss sustained by the McCord Company. She was appalled and sickened by the waste the force of nature had wrought upon the road.

"How can Jed possibly recoup from these losses?" she inquired. "No matter how rich he is, this has to be a blow."

"I don't like being pessimistic, Miss Kelly," Ben answered soberly as he ruffled the thick sheaf of damage reports, "but if Jed doesn't luck out with those bankers in Lexington, he could lose the company."

"I knew it was bad," she said, turning away to hide the ache, knowing the man she loved was facing a bad time and there was nothing she could do to help.

"Now don't go getting upset," Ben drawled. "Jed's pulled this company through worse than this and he'll do it again. So wipe that worried look off your pretty face and fetch me the Conrad files."

Ben's sure confidence in Jed's abilities helped bolster her sagging spirits. She smiled and hurried to bring the file he'd requested. She would try not to worry until she was sure there was something to worry about. But as Ben's attention was buried in the file and she returned to her own work, all her apprehensions returned and she knew that she would never be able to put her concern for Jed aside.

The week passed and still there was no word from Jed. Cindy was tormented by her rapidly growing fears that his appeal to the Lexington bankers had fallen on deaf ears. Daily she reassured herself, keeping the belief alive that he would call at any moment to let them know the loan had gone through. But as the days slipped by her confidence slipped too.

The second week was worse than the first and even Ben was finding it hard to keep his spirits up. "Why the hell doesn't he call?" he muttered, eyeing the silent black telephone.

"Why don't *you* call *him*?" Cindy suggested. "Just to see how things are going."

"I tried that last night," Ben revealed, "but his answering service said he had gone to one of those bankers' parties and he'd left word he wasn't to be disturbed."

"Did you leave word for him to return your call?" Cindy tried to cloak her curiosity behind an in uninterested facade. Ben's usually keen mind was distracted by worry so he didn't seem to notice how eagerly she awaited his answer.

"Yes, I left word. But you know how those parties usually turn out. He's probably out with one of those fancy women of his and he won't get around to calling me until he's good and ready. And only the good Lord knows when that will be!" Ben's agitation was plain as he lifted his cap and ran nervous fingers through his unruly hair. "Sometimes I think women were put on this earth with the sole purpose of driving good men crazy. Begging your pardon, Miss Kelly, present company excepted."

"Does he have lots of women?" she asked, pretending indifference.

"Does he have women!" Ben answered, rolling his eyes and grinning expressively. "He has them crawling out of the woodwork."

"If women like him so well, why hasn't he married?" she asked, her curiosity overcoming her reluctance to encourage Ben's eloquent portrayal of Jed's romances.

"Oh, Jed's too smart for that," Ben laughed. "Why settle for one when you can have them all?"

"A regular Don Juan," Cindy muttered contemptuously. "I've met his type before. They don't make good husbands, so I guess it's a good thing he never married."

"No . . . ." Ben said thoughtfully. "I believe Jed will settle down when he finds the right woman. He likes kids a lot, and I know he wants a son to carry on his name. No, you're wrong, Miss Kelly. Jed will make a great family man."

"Is . . . is there someone special in his life now?" she asked, and her green eyes were dark as she waited for Ben to answer.

"Well," Ben drawled thoughtfully, "there's the banker's daughter. She hangs on to Jed like she owns him. But here lately I kind of got the idea he might be interested in someone else. Jed's pretty close-mouthed about his private affairs, though, so I don't really know."

Cindy sank into her chair as a deep despair engulfed her. Ben's words had struck her with the force of a blow. Never in her wildest dreams had she thought of Jed with another woman, but Ben had painted a vivid picture in her mind, one that she couldn't shake.

Quickly she turned to the papers on her desk as she fought the hot jealousy that threatened to consume her. "Maybe he'll call before long," she said, her voice muffled by the knot that filled her throat.

"Is there something wrong, Miss Kelly?" Ben asked, his attention caught by the odd huskiness of her tone.

"No, I . . . I might be catching cold, but it's nothing serious." She prayed Ben wouldn't pursue this questioning any longer and, after a long searching glance in her direction, he let the matter drop.

Cindy had never had such a long day. It dragged on and on, and still Jed didn't return Ben's call. How could he spend all that time away from his office in Lexington? she fumed to herself. If he lost everything it would be his own fault. Letting his business go while he played around with—in Ben'd words—a fancy woman. The green-eyed monster that raged within her had her totally convinced that Ben's suppositions were correct, and she vowed never to worry about Jed again.

At precisely five o'clock she covered her typewriter, tidied her desk and crossed the street to the hardware store, meeting Arthur at the entrance.

"Now that's what I call timing," she said.

"You're a very rare creature, Cindy," Arthur replied, with a twinkle in his eyes behind the thick glasses. "A woman who's punctual is hard to find."

"Well, I'm looking forward to this evening, Arthur," Cindy said as she smiled at him. Vivid pictures of Jed and the woman filled her mind but she pushed them away. Tonight she would forget Jed McCord; Arthur's warm admiration would be the balm that would help her forget.

"Jan and Hank are coming over later and Mother and Sudie are waiting. Shall we walk?" Arthur asked. "It's only five blocks away."

"Yes, let's do. I've kept them waiting before and I don't want to do *that* again." Cindy's smile was brilliant as she tucked her arm into his.

Arthur's eyes were quizzical and he peered nearsightedly at her. "Is everything all right, Cindy?

You seem so different tonight."

"Yes, I suppose I am different," she admitted as they strolled down the street arm in arm. "Today I put away hopeless dreams and futile expectations. I can't live my life always waiting for something that's never going to happen, so I've decided to enjoy myself."

"It's Jed McCord, isn't it?" Arthur asked slowly. "I knew there was something between the two of you that day out at the cabin. The air was charged with it."

"There's nothing between us but a mutual dislike," Cindy denied hotly. "And I hope I never see him again! He uses people and when he's finished with them, they're forgotten. How could any woman in her right mind want him?"

"I think you're wrong." Arthur stopped and turned to her. "I think you're in love with him and something happened today that has led you to believe it's hopeless. Am I right?"

Wordlessly she nodded, her eyes bright with unshed tears. "I seem to have an unerring penchant for falling in love with selfish men."

"I don't believe McCord was as indifferent as you seem to think," Arthur said, pulling his handkerchief from his breast pocket and dabbing at her wet cheeks. "But if I'm wrong and there isn't any chance of you and McCord getting together, I want you to remember I'll always be here. I know you don't love me, but people have married without being in love before and it's worked. I have enough love for both of us, and I'm sure I could make you happy."

"Oh, Arthur, you're so good. You deserve more." She twisted the damp handkerchief with trembling fingers. "I love you like the brother I never had, and I want you to have *all* that marriage has to offer. You would be cheating yourself if you settled for less."

"Well," he said, "I really didn't think you'd accept, but I didn't lose anything by trying, did I?"

"Arthur, you've gained more than you'll ever know." Cindy's green eyes regarded him warmly. "You'll always have my respect and affection. You've proved there are decent men in this world. I know there's a girl waiting for you, and when you find her you'll be glad I didn't accept you tonight."

"McCord is a bigger fool than I'd thought if he doesn't come back and carry you off to his big estate in Lexington," Arthur said, smiling down at her. "But until that happens, I'll be here with a strong shoulder whenever you need it."

"Thank you. Now, if we don't get going, your mother and Sudie will think I've gotten lost *again*," she reminded him. "And Louise Bains is peeking at us from behind her living-room drapes. We might be the next item to be discussed at the Wednesday Afternoon Garden Club."

Arthur threw back his head and laughed. "That might come as a surprise to Mother. She's the president."

"I didn't know that." Cindy's cheeks were pink as she smiled at his forthright amusement.

"How else do you think I get my news? The Garden Club spreads more information than the newspaper."

"You're worse than Jan," Cindy teased, taking his hand and pulling him down the street. "But in case you're right, I'll act very prim and proper so as not to sully your good name."

"You can sully my good name any time you please," Arthur returned grandly. "But I'm afraid

162

we'll have to put it off for awhile. Mother and Sudie are waiting."

Midway off the quiet tree-lined street, Arthur halted before a huge, stately, two-story white house that was enclosed by a neat picket fence. "This is it," he announced, swinging open the gate.

"Oh, Arthur," Cindy breathed in awe, "it's beautiful, and so big. Do you mean to tell me that only you and your mother live here?"

"Why, this is *tiny* compared to the apartment buildings in Lexington," Arthur laughed, looking down into her eyes. "I'll bet you lived in a larger house than this."

"Yes, but a lot of other people lived there too," Cindy retorted.

"Arthur! Are you going to stand out there swinging on that gate all night? Or are you going to fetch that girl up here and introduce her?" Millie Corry stood in the shadows of the screened porch thumping her cane impatiently. Although she wasn't very tall, her broad commanding figure compelled instant compliance from Arthur.

"Yes, ma, we're coming." He winked at Cindy, "Mother gets testy when she's kept waiting. But don't worry, she's all bark and no bite."

With a tinge of apprehension, Cindy followed Arthur up to the porch and into the presence of the monarch of Pine Valley society.

"Mother, Sudie, this is Cindy Kelly. Cindy, my mother and Sudie Perice." Arthur performed the introductions grandly. "Now that that's over, shall we go inside?"

"Of course. Where are my manners?" Millie said, and as the stern set of her face was broken by a broad smile, Cindy felt all her inhibitions fade.

Flanked by the two elderly women, Cindy was

ushered into a room of breathtaking proportions. The white walls glowed under the mellow light of the crystal chandelier that hung down from the high ceiling, and the deep wine of the carpet and warm tones of the Chippendale furniture enhanced the elegance of the beautiful room. As Cindy's gaze wandered over the marble fireplace, she exclaimed with awe, "Oh, it's so grand!"

"Yes." Millie nodded. "When my husband, the senator, was alive, we entertained constantly and this room was admired by many."

"Arthur's father was a senator?" Cindy asked, overwhelmed.

"Yes, but that was many years ago and we're interested in you. Tell us about yourself. Do you like living in Pine Valley?"

"I don't think I could explain how much I love this town and the country," Cindy replied, "although it's a lot different than what I'd expected when I moved here."

"My dear," Millie said, patting Cindy's hand, "I know exactly how you feel. I traveled to all the glamorous cities of the world with my late husband, but I was never more happy than when we were home, here in Pine Valley. Isn't that right, Sudie?" She turned questioning eyes to the small birdlike lady who sat nodding sagely. "Goodness, Sudie. What's happened to you? You haven't said a word."

"I was just thinking, Millie," Sudie said, her eyes bright in her tiny face, "of how much Cindy reminds me of you at that age. She has the same zest for life, the same fearless way of meeting obstacles head on, and, after seeing that red hair, I guess she probably has the same quick temper."

"Sudie Perice! I have never had any trouble controlling my temper, and you know it." Millie's eyes flashed, and if she'd been speaking to any other woman but Sudie, she would have run for cover.

"Millie, you've never acknowledged your one fault, and you know that," Sudie replied, completely unruffled. "I don't know how you would have made it all these years if you hadn't had me to smooth all the people you upset."

Cindy sat quietly through this heated exchange and she stiffled an impulse to laugh as she realized how Alice must have felt at the Mad Hatter's tea party. Any moment now she expected a large white rabbit to run through the room, moaning because he was late.

"Mother, Sudie." Arthur's voice stopped them before full-scale war erupted. "You promised. No bickering."

"That's true, Millie," Sudie said, nodding at Arthur's mother. "We promised not to embarrass the boy."

"Yes," Millie replied with narrowed eyes and pursed lips, "but we are going to discuss this later." Then she turned to Cindy and, in a surprisingly sweet tone, said, "I'm so glad you came over tonight and I hope *certain people* haven't caused you to form a bad impression of us."

"No, she hasn't . . . uh . . . I mean," Cindy stuttered, and then she smiled. "I'm enjoying my visit."

"Good," Millie said briskly, rising to her feet. "Now I'll get the tea."

"May I help you?" Cindy offered.

"No, thank you, dear. Sudie will help. I don't dare leave her here. She'll tell *all* my faults and I wouldn't want anyone to know *all* of them."

Bickering happily, the two departed into the

165

recesses of the house, their voices filtering faintly back to the parlor before the closing of a door shut them off.

"What can I say?" Arthur grinned wryly.

"Don't say anything," she replied. "I think they're marvelous. Anyone can see that it's all a game to them. I'm glad I came."

"You're very perceptive," he said, admiringly. "I'm glad you came too. Your smile has brightened the whole room."

"I'm happy to have something to smile about," she said. "The flood has caused so many problems. I admire the people here for the way they united to help the victims of the high water. I never knew a whole town could work together so well and so fast. Most of the people who were flooded out of their homes have been relocated and the cleanup has started. It won't be long before everything will be as it was before."

"Well, not everything," Arthur said solemnly. "Some things can never be replaced, but we'll do what we can. But what about the McCord Company? Were the damages as bad as was feared?"

"It was terrible," Cindy admitted. "Ben and I don't know for sure how the company has fared. Jed had meetings scheduled with the Lexington bankers last week, but so far we haven't received any word on how they went."

"Don't look so worried, Cindy," Arthur soothed, "I'm sure the road will be completed. Too much has been invested in it for it to fall through now."

"Oh, I'm not worried about that," Cindy answered. "I know the road will go on. I just don't know if the McCord Company will be the one who finishes it."

"You can set your mind to rest, young lady,"

Millie Corry said matter of factly as she wheeled a tea trolley, complete with a silver service, into the room. "The McCord Company goes back to work Monday morning."

"How do you know that?" Cindy asked, dumbfounded. "There has been no word at the office. At least there wasn't when I left at five o'clock."

"Oh, I imagine Mr. Kendrick has heard by now," Millie murmured, with a complacent expression.

"I don't understand." Cindy remained bewildered. How could these two possibly know something that she and Ben hadn't been able to find out, even with phone calls?

"All right, Mother!" Arthur admonished. "You've kept us dangling long enough. How do you know?"

Cindy was grateful for Arthur's intervention. She was on pins and needles waiting for Millie's answer. She only hoped it was true.

"It's very simple, Arthur," his mother said patiently. "Louise Bain called just before you and Cindy came. She said the road crew superintendent called and booked all the rooms at the motel. They'll be here Monday."

"Well then," Arthur said, "if that's true, I guess the McCord Company is back in business."

"Of course it's true," Millie snapped. "You don't think Louise Bain lied, do you?"

"Now, now," Sudie tutted, waving a skinny finger at Millie, "what did you say about your temper?"

"I did not lose my temper," Millie replied in a quieter tone, although she continued to rattle the tea service alarmingly. "I merely pointed out that, as Louise and Merle Bain own the motel, they should know when someone books all the rooms."

"You snapped at Arthur and you know it, Millie," Sudie replied stubbornly.

"I did not!" Millie blustered.

"You did too!" This time Sudie wasn't going to give in.

"Mrs. Corry, Miss Perice," Cindy broke in, "thank you for the information. It really has relieved my mind."

Both women forgot the argument as they smiled at Cindy.

"Think nothing of it, my dear." Sudie was all sweetness and light. "And Cindy, I did want to say that you're even more beautiful than I'd thought."

"Now what has that got to do with the conversation?" Millie asked sharply as she eyed Sudie with suspicion.

"Nothing. I just wanted to change the subject." Sudie giggled.

"Yes, I guess we should." Millie turned up her nose at Sudie. "And for once she's right. You are very pretty, my dear."

At that moment the doorbell chimed and Cindy was glad of the respite as Millie excused herself and went to answer. Out in the hall she heard Jan's familiar voice and smiled as she heard the reproach in Milie's voice. "Jan Jenkins, I'm surprised you decided to come see us. You haven't been here for awhile."

Her thoughts returned to the information Millie had relayed. The road crew was returning. That meant Jed's meetings had been successful. With distaste she wondered to what lengths he'd gone in order to save his company. She hoped she'd never know.

"Hi, Cindy," Jan greeted as she bounced into the room. "You look dazed. Have these two been too

168

much for you?"

The two to whom she referred beamed at the vivacious girl and she grinned fondly at them.

"What? Oh, no, I've enjoyed my visit," Cindy replied, although her mind was still on Jed and the company.

"Would you like some tea, Jan?" Sudie asked, reaching for the silver pot.

"No thanks, Sudie. Hank is waiting outside," Jan told her. "We thought Arthur and Cindy might want to go out for dinner and a movie tonight."

At Arthur's questioning look, Cindy nodded. "Yes, let's do. I think it would be fun."

"Jan, we just managed to get this elusive girl over for a visit and you come in and rush her away!" Millie cried, as she frowned in Jan's direction.

"And we were so enjoying the visit, too," Sudie joined in.

"Hey, don't be downcast. I was just going to ask if we could drop by Sunday," Jan soothed diplomatically. "I want to show you some sketches of my wedding dress and Cindy will need some advice concerning her gown. Sudie is the best seamstress in town." This was directed to Cindy. "And I'll want her opinion on everything."

"Oh, Jan," Sudie breathed, clasping her hands together and looking more like a sparrow than ever, "I'd love to see the sketches."

"Well," Millie said, only slightly mollified, "all right, if you promise to come Sunday, after church."

"We promise!" both girls answered in unison.

"Okay, then, let's go," Arthur said as he ushered them from the parlor and through the door. "I'll bring my car around and you go tell Hank we'll take that. There's not enough room for all four of us in the pickup."

"I'm glad to hear you say that." Jan grinned, her freckles dancing. "The last time four of us took the truck, Hank almost broke my leg with the floor shift."

"Be right out." Arthur laughed, heading for the garage.

"I think you were a hit," Jan commented, as they walked down the sidewalk to Hank's truck. "They really hated to see you leave."

"I don't know why," Cindy remarked, "I didn't say much."

"You didn't have to. You came to see them and that was enough." Jan smiled. "A lot of girls wouldn't have taken the time."

The four friends piled into Arthur's car and drove down to the diner. After hamburgers and cokes, they went over to Bradford to the drive-in movie. The evening was filled with laughter and merriment and Cindy was glad she'd agreed to go, although occasionally her thoughts returned to Jed McCord. But when this happened, she'd remember the promise she had made to herself and that was enough to erase him from her mind.

Finally the time came to say goodnight and, as Cindy and Jan watched from the darkness of the porch, Arthur's big car pulled onto the highway and headed back to town.

"Oh, Cindy," Jan sighed, staring out into the still night, "I wish you were as happy as I am. Oh you do a good job of hiding it, but I know you still want that big galoot Jed McCord. Arthur is mighty interested in you, though I know he isn't handsome or even particularly witty, but he would make a fine husband."

"Arthur proposed tonight," Cindy confided, as she sank into the porch swing.

"I knew it. I knew it!" Jan exclaimed, turning to Cindy, happiness sparkling in her big brown eyes. "Well?"

"Jan, I can't marry Arthur. I don't love him." Cindy's tone was anguished. "I seem to love men who don't return the feelings. Maybe that's the way it'll always be."

"Well," Jan sighed, "I had hoped that Arthur would make you forget Jed McCord, although I should've known that wouldn't happen. Are you sure you aren't transferring your feelings from Brent to Jed? After all, you're just getting over one bad experience with a man; maybe you've allowed this to affect how you feel about McCord."

"I wish that were true," Cindy revealed. "But Ben was talking about Jed today and I realized my feelings were deeper than I knew. I guess romance isn't for me." She laughed bitterly. "Maybe I'll be like Sudie Perice and never get married. I'll just stay around and be your old maid best friend forever."

"I know all this looks bad right now," Jan comforted her, "but who knows, maybe the road construction will begin again and McCord will return to Pine Valley."

"Oh, it's starting again Monday." Cindy grinned in spite of herself. "Guess how I know?"

"The Wednesday Afternoon Garden Club!" Jan guessed.

"That's right." Cindy burst out laughing. "I'll never doubt you again. They do know everything . . . and I mean everything!"

THIRTEEN

At the stroke of eight Cindy entered the McCord field office and saw Ben grinning jauntily from his position in a dangerously tipped office chair.

"Careful," she warned dryly. "You could fall and break your neck."

"Where were you last night?" he inquired, as the legs of the chair hit the floor with a resounding thud. "I called several times but you weren't home."

"I went to a movie; but I know what you wanted to tell me," Cindy replied calmly, as she removed the dust cover from her typewriter. "Jed McCord has landed on his feet one more time."

"Yep. 'Course I never doubted him. That boy could charm the birds out of a tree. Those Lexington bankers never had a chance," Ben crowed enthusiastically. "Yes, ma, we're back in business."

Cindy's response was noncommittal as she straightened papers and then sharpened a pencil. "I wonder what he did to bring those bankers around."

"Anything it took, I imagine," Ben said, missing the look that crossed Cindy's face. "The company is very important to him. He built it from nothing after he returned from the Army and Vietnam. I don't think he's prepared to let it go without a fight."

"You paint a very ruthless picture of him," she commented coolly.

"Jed is a man's man and I wouldn't want to be the person who stands between him and something he wants. No sir." Ben's praise had caused Cindy's temper to rise.

"Do you mean that when I refused to sell my property, I was risking the great Jed McCord's wrath?" she asked hotly.

"Let's just say I was glad you gave in when you did." Ben chuckled. "Although it would have been something to see if you two had clashed. I don't think I've ever seen a woman stand up to him the way you have. I'll never forget his face the day you poured the water over his head. I thought he would have a stroke." Ben guffawed at the memory.

"I wish I'd done worse," Cindy muttered, seething. "I suppose now he'll be returning to Pine Valley to run his precious company."

"Oh, eventually. But it'll be awhile. He still has business in Lexington."

"Monkey business, no doubt," Cindy said grimly.

Ben turned and stared at Cindy, questions in his eyes. "Is something wrong? You don't seem happy at the news and yesterday you were so worried. Has something happened that I haven't heard?"

"No, nothing's happened," Cindy said. "I was out late last night and it's made me grumpy. I'm glad for you and the company, Ben." She inserted paper into the typewriter. "Now let's get to work before the boss fires us both."

"Yes, we should manage to look busy. He's coming down this afternoon to look at the damage reports." With that piece of nerve-shattering news Ben turned back to the reports on his desk.

Cindy's first thought was to flee the office. Surely she could think of some excuse. Maybe an emergency at home. No, she wasn't going to run any more. She'd stay and be poised and calm. She would never be able to hold this job if she ran away every time Jed came into the office. She'd show him that he had absolutely no effect on her at all. And with these mental resolutions she tried to bury herself in her work. But every time a car passed outside her heart would pound and she'd dart a quick peek at Ben to see if he had noticed anything amiss.

When Jed did open the office door later that afternoon, she was totally unprepared. Ben had left the office a few minutes before to check supplies in the supply yard out back. She was engrossed in rearranging the scattered files, down on her knees, her nose buried deep in the bottom drawer, and she hadn't heard the truck stop outside.

"Well, it's nice to see that you're still hard at work," Jed's deep-timbered voice drawled, causing her back to stiffen.

Electric feelings flashed through her body and she fought to control all traces of this as she swiveled on her heels and looked up into his mocking gray eyes. Slowly his gaze traveled over her face and down her body, and she felt a flame flicker in the pit of her stomach. Her green eyes were betraying her feelings, so she quickly hid her expression behind lowered lashes.

"Ben's out in the supply yard," she said quickly,

getting to her feet. "I'll go get him."

"No rush." Jed grinned, displaying his even white teeth, "Here's someone I want you to meet." He reached behind his broad back and pulled a sleek blonde girl into view. "Charleen Farrel, Cindy Kelly," he said, wasting no words on the introduction, and then he turned to the stack of reports on Ben's desk.

Cindy glared at his wide shoulders and then hastily rearranged her features as she turned and smiled at the sultry Charleen. "Hello," she said extending her hand, but she withdrew it with haste as she noticed the girl's slight grimace of distaste. Looking down, she saw that her hands were smudged with dust she'd collected while re-arranging the files. Embarrassed, she rubbed her hands down the sides of her jeans and eyed the girl who had accompanied Jed on his trip to Pine Valley.

Charleen's stunning blonde beauty was equalled only by her air of cold superiority. As she tilted her thin aristocratic nose and gathered her expensive mink coat to her slim body, Cindy had an almost irresistible urge to walk out of the office. She felt a strong aversion to the girl and she knew she wasn't being fair. But as Charleen spoke, she realized her first instincts had been true.

"My goodness, darling, are dungarees the proper uniform for office work?" Charleen inquired in a haughty manner.

"I never know when I might be required to go out to one of the road sites," Cindy replied, shooting a hostile glare at Jed's suspiciously still back. "Nice clothes can be ruined very quickly out there."

"Oh dear, you girls who work for a living do

have it bad," Charleen said, her voice dripping with sympathy. "I really do have to admire you. Why, my daddy would never allow me to dress like that, much less work in a place like this. Jed darling, can't you do anything to brighten this place up? Maybe an interior decorator? This is terrible."

"Charleen, honey, this is a field office," Jed replied, smiling indulgently at her outspoken disdain. "Its sole purpose is work. If I want comfort I'll go to my office in Lexington."

"But Jed, what about this poor girl? She has to work in all this squalor," she protested sweetly, waving ring-laden fingers in Cindy's direction.

"I haven't heard Miss Kelly complain," Jed said, hooking a long leg on the edge of the desk and sitting there. "Do you want to complain?" he asked, turning a mocking gaze in Cindy's direction.

"This office suits me fine," she snapped. "Besides, I'll be moving into my own office as soon as Mr. Ames finds one."

"Ah yes. You see, Charleen, Miss Kelly doesn't work for the McCord Company. She's here with us in conjunction with the Ames Agency. So any time she doesn't like the conditions around here, she can demand a plush office all her own."

"Then, my dear, that's what you must do. Immediately." Charleen was very pleased as she tried to convince Cindy of her concern for her welfare. "I'm sure your employer would move you out of here at once if he could only see where you work."

"I'm fine, and I don't think complaining will make an office pop out of nowhere," Cindy answered. "As a matter of fact, Mr. Ames has just about decided to buy a lot here in town and build an office, so I'll have to made do with this little desk until then."

"I'm sure if you talked with him he could rent something suitable," Charleen persisted.

Cindy was puzzled. It was plain the girl wanted her out of the office, and then she understood. Charleen was afraid Jed would be spending too much time in Pine Valley; she was trying to keep the two of them apart. Well, her fears were groundless, Cindy mused, because she posed no competition for the girl. She'd have thought Charleen would have known it, just by the way Jed treated her.

"But I suppose you country girls are quite hardy," Charleen said, her blue eyes like frosted glass. "I imagine you're accustomed to squalid conditions such as these."

Cindy's color was high as she turned away, gritting her teeth. Her small hands were clenched and she fought to control her anger. Never had another woman infuriated her more. But no matter how much she was provoked, she was determined to keep her temper under control. She pasted a cool smile on her lips and, as their eyes met, she was surprised at the frankly appraising gaze she encountered. But Charleen's expression quickly changed; an icy mask descended, hiding her thoughts.

"Excuse me," Cindy muttered. "I'll go find Ben." With her head held high she brushed past Charleen and went out, slamming the door behind her. She slipped her hands in the back pockets of her jeans and shook her long red curls disgustedly as she sauntered down to the supply yard.

Cindy presented a very dejected picture as she leaned against a tall stack of lumber and watched silently as Ben worked on his inventory of the supplies.

"We need to get an order out today if we're resuming construction Monday," Ben announced, tapping his pen on the clipboard he held. "We don't have enough supplies to last a week."

"You can discuss that with the boss," Cindy said, wrinkling her nose and gesturing over her shoulder toward the office. "He's up there. And be forewarned, he isn't alone."

"Well, I'd best be getting up there," Ben said. "I'll finish this inventory later."

"Oh, I'll do it," she said, reaching for the clipboard. "I'm finished with the files and this needs to be done."

"Are you sure?" Ben asked. "You don't have to. It's not part of your job, you know."

"I'd love to do it." Cindy grinned; she'd never meant anything more. "You tend to the boss and his friend. I'll be fine."

With deep relief she watched Ben hurry to the office. Just as she turned away she noticed Jed watching them from the window. Although he was some distance away, she saw that a deep scowl twisted his features. Maybe that creature is getting to him too, she mused, a bitter taste in her mouth. I sure hope so.

She put the occupants of the office out of her mind as she began the routine counting of supplies. With agility she climbed from lumber piles and rows of sewer pipe to sacks of concrete, jotting the numbers on the sheet as she worked.

The sun was low as she stood on widespread legs and eyed the last huge stack of lumber. Just this pile and she would be done, she thought, kicking a rock out of her way. Then what would she do? Jed's truck remained parked in the lot, though she'd put off this stack hoping he'd take his friend and go before she had to return to the office.

Might as well get it done, she decided, then she'd drop off the clipboard and head for home.

"Are you going to hide out here all night?" Jed's tone was amused as he stood leaning against the boards she was counting.

"I'm almost finished," she answered, avoiding his eyes as she continued her work. "And just what makes you think I'm hiding?"

"Well," he drawled, his gray eyes gleaming, "a time or two there I thought I detected a few sparks between you and Charleen."

"A woman like that isn't worth wasting sparks on," Cindy spat at him, "although she does suit you to a tee. But be careful; I don't think she's the kind to be satisfied with momentary pleasures. She and her banker daddy may end up owning you body and soul."

"What makes you think her father's a banker?" Jed inquired, a pleased, self-satisfied look on his face.

"Well, he is, isn't he?" she demanded irritably. "And what are you looking so smug about?"

"Well, if I didn't know you so well, Spitfire," he said, moving toward her, "I'd think you were jealous."

"You'd better think again," she retorted sharply. As he straightened, she backed away. "There's nothing to be jealous of."

Her back was against the lumber and she could retreat no further. Wide eyed, she stared up at his tall form and raised her arms to keep him at bay. "Don't push me like this," she warned, fighting the warm rush of feeling that threatened to send her into his arms.

"I'm not pushing," he murmured softly as he stared hungrily into her eyes. "I haven't touched you. I'm just looking."

"Don't look at me like that," she whispered, wetting her dry lips with the tip of her tongue. "I don't like it."

"Are you deliberately trying to make me lose control?" His voice was husky as he bent and lightly claimed her mouth. And as his kiss deepened, Cindy shuddered under a barrage of soulshaking sweetness. With a will of their own, her arms encircled his neck and her fingers lightly fondled his hair. Breathlessly she sighed and returned his kiss, dreading the moment when he would let her go.

"Hum . . . hum . . . . " Ben's cough broke them apart. "Excuse me . . . I . . . I . . . " he stuttered, "Jed, your friend is getting restless. She sent me to find you."

"Oh hell," Jed growled, running his hand through his tousled black hair and glaring at Ben. "Can't you keep her occupied for awhile?"

"He did his best, darling," Charleen's cool voice answered lightly. "You should have told me you were coming down here for a quick grapple behind the lumber pile with the hired help. I wouldn't have sent him down."

Cindy stared at the coldly commanding girl standing there and she could see Jed's loan going down the drain. She had to do something to salvage the situation and there was only one thing that would work.

Stiffening her slender frame, she smiled coolly, hiding her heartbreak. "That's all it was, Miss

Farrel, and I hope that it remains quiet. You see I'm engaged to be married and I don't think my fiance would be as understanding as you."

She flinched as Jed turned a cold contemptuous gaze upon her. As a muscle flickered in his strong jaw, she shrank from the fury that darkened his eyes. He reached for her and his intentions were violent.

"Hold it, Jed," Ben said, moving between the two of them. "Get him out of here, Miss Farrel!"

"Yes, get me out of here, Miss Farrel," Jed said between clenched teeth, "before I do something that I might regret."

Cindy had watched the truck roar down the street before her composure deserted her, leaving her trembling like a frail leaf in a strong wind.

Ben shook his head, muttering, as he stared at the dust in the distance. "I've never seen him like that. Never! He didn't hurt you, did he, Miss Kelly?"

"No, no," Cindy said. She was defeated. "Not where it shows, anyway."

Ben was confused, but his face softened as he saw the state Cindy was in. Helplessly he extended his hand. "Come on, let's go back to the office."

"I guess we might as well," she agreed softly, rubbing her tired neck and turning to hide her misery.

"By the way," Ben said, trying to take her mind off the ugly scene that had just taken place, "you didn't tell me you were engaged."

"I'm not. I just thought that was an easy way to save Jed's loan."

"Save Jed's loan?" Now Ben was really confused. "How could that save Jed's loan?"

"Oh, Ben, she's the banker's daughter," Cindy

181

said, depression draining the life from her voice. "Do I have to spell it out?"

"Do you mean to tell me that you think Jed would resort to shining up to the banker's daughter in order to secure a loan?" Ben was outraged, but then he began to chuckle. "Ah, now I get it. But tell me, just when did you two get together?"

"We are not together," Cindy denied. "He hates me and I . . . I . . . don't care for him either." But the sudden trembling of her lips and the tears that welled in her hurt green eyes gave the lie to her words.

"How two people can get their lives in such a mess is beyond me!" Ben snorted in disgust. "You two hotheads can't even fall in love like normal people."

"Jed McCord is definitely not in love!" Cindy countered dully.

"No? Old Jed may not want to admit it, but he's in love." Ben laughed, slapping his leg. "Damned if I haven't waited a long time for this to happen and I'm going to have a field day rubbing it in."

"If you ever dare mention any of this to Jed or anyone, I'll quit this job and this town and I'll never return," Cindy said, forcing a coldness into her words as she never had before. "Please don't make me leave, Ben, because I truly want to stay."

"You don't mean that, Miss Kelly," he protested, the smile fading from his face. "You two should be together and you could be if you'll let me tell him the truth."

"He doesn't want me and I have my pride. Now promise me, Ben," she said, meeting his wavering gaze with firm resolve. "Promise me!"

"Aw . . . all right, I promise, but only because I

don't want you to leave town. But I still think you're being foolish."

"I'd rather be foolish than rejected again," she said, opening the door. "Now I think I'll go home."

FOURTEEN

After their encounter in the supply yard Jed didn't return to Pine Valley. He managed the business in Lexington and the road work was delegated to Ben. Cindy was buried in mountains of work, brought on by the resumption of the road construction crews. But she was grateful to be busy. It helped keep her mind off things that were best forgotten.

The long hard hours of work revolved into days and the days sped into weeks. Suddenly it was the middle of November and the cold dismal days of winter were upon them.

Gradually Cindy's life had settled into a routine and, although she couldn't claim complete happiness, she was content with the quiet country life and her job. She had begun to feel she was a part of the small town and was glad that she had moved to the valley.

Then came the end of November. Thanksgiving was over and the bleak countryside was covered with a smooth white blanket of snow.

Cindy awoke early that morning and as she gazed out the window she was enchanted by the Christmas card beauty of the landscape.

"Oh, Jan," she cried, "the snow must be very

deep. The rosebush is completely covered."

"Yes, I know, and I have an appointment with Sudie today. She's starting my dress and I don't know if I can make it to town or not." Jan was crestfallen. The gown was all she'd talked about for weeks and, now that Sudie had agreed to be her seamstress, she was anxious to get started.

"You'll make it," Cindy replied, her eyes still on the view. "A roadgrader just went up, so the highway is clear."

"Good!" Jan was delighted. "Come with me, Cindy. Sudie really likes you and Millie will probably be there too."

"I like them too, but today is Saturday and I think I'll catch up on my share of the housework. You have been saddled with most of it lately, you know. And then I might take a walk. The office has been hectic this week and I'll enjoy a rest." Cindy's tone was quiet but firm, and Jan knew she wouldn't be swayed by arguments, but she tried anyway.

"You'll need to pick out your dress. After all, you *are* my Maid of Honor," Jan reminded her.

"Jan, the wedding isn't until June! I have loads of time," Cindy said, laughing at her friend.

Jan finally left and Cindy started clearing the breakfast dishes from the table. An hour later she stood at the kitchen sink and listlessly washed the dishes as she gazed out the small window at the smooth white snow that blanketed the ground. She wanted to leave the mundane household chores that had accumulated during the week and walk the paths she'd discovered in the forest behind the barn. Her solitary walks always calmed her troubled mind and the only really contented moments she had now were while she roamed the quiet woods alone.

With determination she put her desires aside and started the laundry. She would finish her work; then the rest of the day would be hers. Hopefully she'd be out of the house before Jan returned for, though her intentions were good, Cindy would welcome a respite from her chatter.

After a tuna fish sandwich and a glass of milk for lunch, Cindy leaned back and glanced with satisfaction around the sparkling clean house. Now all she had to do was change her clothes and get away before Jan returned.

She took a quick shower, then pulled on her denim jeans and an ivory turtleneck sweater. She brushed out her red-gold curls and pulled a bulky ivory knit toboggan cap down over her ears. A green ski jacket and black hiking boots completed her outfit, but she flung a green scarf around her neck for extra warmth before she hurried from the room.

The smooth surface of the snow was soon broken by Cindy's tracks as she plowed across the yard and waded the drifts beside the old barn. When she entered the silent forest, she drew a deep breath of appreciation of the pristine beauty that surrounded her.

Snow clung to the branches of the trees and some of the evergreens were bent almost to the ground under the weight. The sun sparkling across the blinding whiteness creating a fairyland. The chattering of the gray squirrel that lived in the old hickory nut tree drew her attention as she watched him scold the brilliant red cardinal that perched inquisitively on the branch above him. She shook her head at his antics and watched as the beautiful bird disdainfully soared away with a flutter of red wings.

She turned from the foul-tempered little king of the forest and, with a sigh shook the snow from the small evergreen, allowing it to straighten up once more.

"Hello, Spitfire," Jed's richly timbered voice came from behind her.

Cindy's heart lurched painfully as she turned with disbelief and saw his tall masculine figure advancing on her. She swallowed convulsively. "What are you doing here?" Her stomach contracted sharply and his keen piercing eyes held her hypnotized.

"I came to see how you were getting along," he drawled. "Ben tells me you're the best help I'd ever hired, and that's only a part of what he had to say." Tall and darkly handsome, he stood there in the snow, a lock of dark hair across his tanned forehead.

"You talked to Ben about me?" She spoke stiffly, aware of the weakness in her knees as she wondered how much longer she could stand there under his mesmerizing gaze.

"Would you mind telling me just how you got the idea that by telling Charleen you were engaged, you were protecting my bank loans?" he asked, pinning her down with narrowed gray eyes.

"I . . . I didn't want her to get the wrong idea about us. She might have gotten her father to change his mind about the loan. Anyone could see she considered you her own exclusive property," she said in a rush.

"Lord deliver me from the logic of a woman," Jed muttered beseechingly as he threw up his hands. "First of all, I was a damned fool. I brought Charleen to Pine Valley for one reason: to make you jealous. If it worked then I would know for sure you cared for me. But that backfired, as you know. Second, I do not romance bankers' daughters to secure loans. I hope I'm above that. The loan had nothing to do with Charleen. And third," he added, advancing on her, "I should beat you for the hell you put me through these last few weeks."

"I imagine it wasn't too great a hell," she retorted bitterly. "Not when you had Charleen to console you."

"I haven't seen her since that day in Pine Valley," Jed replied, a satisfied expression in his eyes. "I think she realized where my feelings lay and started looking for brighter prospects."

Cindy couldn't believe what he seemed to be saying and this time she was determined to escape unscathed. She wouldn't allow him to toy with her emotions any more.

"I . . . I . . . have to go!" She rubbed her hands on her sides. "Jan is expecting me back at the house," she said in a rush.

"No she isn't." Jed smiled as the distance closed between them. "I saw Jan in town and she said not to expect her until late."

"You talked to Jan, too," Cindy whispered from frozen lips.

"Yes, I talked to her," he admitted, although he didn't act as if he intended to repeat the conversation. "Are you afraid of me?" he asked, as she backed away from him.

"No." She shook her head, but the denial was a lie.

"Then stop backing away!" he said harshly, a muscle leaping in his jaw. "What's happened to the spitfire that I left?"

"Nothing's happened to me," she flashed, as her temper rose. "What do you want with me?"

"I want to marry you!" His voice was pure steel and a dangerous light flickered in his gray eyes. "Don't say a word. I don't care if you're engaged or not! I don't care if you feel something for the lawyer, either. I'm going to marry you no matter *how* many men there are in your life."

Cindy's green eyes were wide and a wavering laugh broke from her throat. She glanced wildly around, trying to find an avenue of escape.

Jed's hands gripped her shoulders firmly. "No matter how you feel about those other men, there's a magnetism between us that you can't deny. I love you and I can't live without you." His fingers tangled in her shining red-gold curls and his mouth covered hers in a deeply possessive and searching kiss.

The ground tilted beneath her feet and she responded with all the love that was in her. Her arms twined around his neck and she held him close to her heart.

His lips came away from her mouth, although he still held her within his iron grip. "I wanted to do that as soon as I saw you the first time," he murmured huskily. "Tell me the truth—you can feel the sparks too, can't you?"

"Yes, oh yes," she whispered, joy singing through her veins.

"Tell me you'll marry me." His old arrogance was surfacing once mòre. "Tell me you *love* me!"

"Oh yes, I love you." Cindy smiled mistily. "I love you and I'll marry you. There is no man in my life but you."

"I've been going out of my mind picturing you and that playboy you met at the motel together, and now you tell me there is no one else. Where is he?" Jed's tone was bewildered as he held her tightly.

"He went back to Lexington a few minutes after you did, I suppose," she said, smiling up into his searching gray eyes. "I sent him away."

"You sent him away. . . ." Jed's voice was unbelieving as he saw the truth shining from her black-lashed emerald eyes. "You sent him away and all this time I thought. . . ."

Anger flashed into the green eyes that had just been shining with love. She put her hands against his broad chest and shoved him away.

"You thought what?" she asked, her cheeks flushed.

"You said you were experienced, and what I saw you meeting him at the motel I believed you. I've been crazy, wanting you and despising you at the same time. I'm so jealous of the men you spend time with that I can't bear having you out of my sight." Jed's voice was ragged and low.

"And you believed I was meeting him at the motel so we could . . . we could. . . ." She couldn't bring herself to put into words the thoughts Jed had carried back to Lexington that day. And it had been because of her claims that night at the cabin. "I lied to you that night at the cabin. I wanted one night with you, but you'd said you were only interested in women of experience, so I lied. But you *still* turned me away. I could have died of humiliation," she cried angrily, as she dashed the tears from her cheeks. "Now you say you'll take me even though I'm slightly used! No thanks, Jed McCord. I don't want you! Now get out of my life and leave me alone!"

Sobbing bitterly, she ran from him through the

powdery snow. With a flying tackle, Jed sent her sprawling into a deep drift. She pummeled his strong arms as she tried to evade his grasp. "Let me go," she wailed, gasping for breath. "I hate you, and if you don't let me go you'll be sorry!"

"Now that's more like the old spitfire." Jed grinned, his gray eyes amuse. "There for a minute I was afraid you'd lost your spirit."

Cindy stiffened in rage as he held her in his grip. Her wide green eyes burned resentfully as she glared up at him.

"Did you really think I'd let you go again?" His voice was lazy as he slowly bent his head to hers. His lean dark face filled her vision and, against her will, she lowered her lashes as his lips met hers with sweet tenderness. She was helpless against the warm, joyful response that sang in her blood, and a rush of love made her want to weep again.

Jed's mouth left hers and as she opened her eyes, she saw him regarding her with lazy satisfaction. "I was right," he said in a husky murmur, "you do love me! And you feel the same hot flash of fire every time we touch."

"Don't take this too seriously," she replied, still trying to deny the truth of his words. "Maybe I respond to all men this way."

A muscle twitched in his firm jaw and a coldness crept into his gray eyes as he looked down at her. "Careful," he warned, his eyes frosty. "I deserved that this time, but don't ever say it again."

"I'll say what I please when I please!" Cindy retorted mulishly as she renewed her struggles to break free.

Her sweet-smelling hair brushed his face and, with a ragged sigh, he said, "I love you and I intend to marry you. I won't let you go until you say yes!"

"Never!" She couldn't bring herself to forget the new hurt he'd caused and her stubborn pride held back the acceptance she wanted to give.

"Our tempers cause us both to say and do things we regret later, but I won't give you up now. Our marriage will be stormy but exciting. You'll have to resign yourself, Cindy Spitfire Kelly. I'm going to be your husband, and if you don't give me the answer I want before long, I won't be responsible for my actions right here in this snow!" His voice was husky as his warm breath touched the nape of her neck. His lips were soft and tender as he found her mouth. The familiar embers started to burn once again and she succumbed to the desire within her.

"I do love you," she whispered. "Yes . . . yes, I'll be your wife." And as she closed her eyes and gave herself to the deep joy of his kiss, she knew within her happy heart that some dreams do come true.